Passion in the Cards

An Opposites-Attract Metaphysical Beach Town Romance

Sadira Stone

Passion in the Cards

♥

Headstrong, homebody farmer plus freedom-loving hippie chick equals the worst match ever, but their blazing chemistry is unstoppable.

Jesse Del Toro struggles to keep his organic farm afloat—hard enough without the delicious, dangerous distraction of Gemma's return to Trappers Cove. The bewitching vagabond will never settle down in his quirky beach town. But once ignited, their fiery attraction sets them on a collision course that could wreck him.

Nursing a wounded heart, Gemma Moore hopes a spell in her Aunt Zora's metaphysical shop will soothe her stormy emotions. But from the moment Jesse walks in, calm is a lost cause. The hunky farmer is frustrating, stubborn, and oh so tempting. One hot night reveals his hidden side—sweet, sensual, and determined to make her his.

When a harmless secret backfires, Gemma discovers just how deeply she's wounded the beautiful bull man, and how desperately she wants to keep him.

Quality Control: I strive to produce error-free books, but even with all the critique partners, beta readers, and editors, sometimes an error slips through. Pretty please, if you find a typo or formatting issue, let me know at sadirastoneauthor@gmail.com so I may correct it. Thank you!

Contents

Chapter One

♥

Her brow scrunched in frustration, Gemma plucked a selenite wand from behind a grinning happy Buddha. "Honestly, Auntie Z, you've got to organize your crystals. They're scattered all over the shop."

Gemma's aunt, proprietor of Madame Zora's Psychic Emporium, shrugged and resumed dusting the dragon figurines, her wide hips and dangly earrings swaying to her beloved Arabian flute music. "I always find what I'm looking for—eventually."

"Gah!" On her last visit to Trappers Cove, Gemma had completely reorganized the shop, and now look at it—a total hodgepodge of incense burners, statuettes, T-shirts, hippie skirts, daggers, candles, and other metaphysical accoutrements. How did customers ever find anything in this magpie's nest?

She lifted a hunk of storm cloud-gray labradorite to the light and admired its rainbow iridescence. A few deep, centering breaths, and the tightness behind her brow eased. Maybe arranging the tchotchkes would help her coax her own rainbow from the dark clouds hanging over her life. This kitschy little beach town on the Washington coast always served up fresh insight. Easier to breathe here, away from Caleb, his new girlfriend, and all the friends who'd taken his side.

She moved to the register. "How about we clear this display case and put the crystals here? That way, you can keep an eye on them. I'll bet a lot of these end up in shoplifters' pockets."

Zora shrugged again. "If someone needs a stone that badly, let 'em have it."

Gemma blew an errant curl off her forehead. "Honestly, Auntie. It's a wonder you even keep the doors open." Good thing her most recent consulting gig ended last week. Zora's business was in dire straits.

The brass bell above the entrance tinkled as Marquetta, Zora's wife, bustled through with three to-go cups and a paper sack. "Holy cats, it's blowing something fierce today." She set her load on the counter and retied her wind-loosened scarf. "Coffee break. Brought you crullers from Cassie's."

"Mmm. They're still warm." Gemma helped herself. Seattle's trendy doughnut shops couldn't touch the crispy, sugary perfection of Cassie's crullers. "Thanks, Auntie M."

"I like to stretch my legs on my break." Chuckling, she leaned in close to Gemma's ear. "Besides, you're gonna need fuel to sort out this jumble."

Zora socked her wife's arm playfully. "Watch yourself, Madam. This is a spiritual space. We don't want your Dewey Decimal uptightness in here."

"Well, you need some kind of system, Auntie." Gemma nudged a coffee across the counter.

"Listen to your niece, babe." Marquetta pecked Zora's cheek. "She always has good ideas. See you at dinnertime. There's lentil stew in the Crockpot." She let herself out and strode toward the library, her long woolen coat flapping in the wintery wind.

"She's right, you know." Zora set down her feather duster and pried the lid from her coffee. "You do have good ideas, dear. I'm glad you were able to clear your schedule for your old auntie."

Sweet of Zora to pretend this visit was about prepping for next month's Esoteric Arts Expo and not about Gemma's recent breakup. Typical Zora—endlessly kind, with an eerie sense of when to press and when to back off.

Zora reached up to dust a set of wind chimes, making the delicate metal tubes tinkle like fairy song. "Customers are always thin after the holidays," she said with a sigh. "This time of year, I've got more bills than profits. I really need to knock that expo out of the ballpark."

Gemma's lips stretched in a fond smile as she hugged her aunt's shoulders. "We'll put together a display so alluring, no one will be able to pass your stand without buying something."

Zora chuckled up at her. "Will you wear that witchy dress you wore last time?"

"The green one? Perhaps. I picked up a new outfit in Eugene, before..." Releasing Zora, she took another bite of pastry to push down the lump rising in her throat, but the treat turned to sawdust in her mouth.

Zora patted her shoulder. "You going to tell me what really brought you here, hon?"

Gemma busied herself arranging crystals. "Oh, you know me. Itchy feet."

"Some tea tree oil will help with that."

"Ha ha." She snatched the feather duster from her aunt's hand and attacked the sparkly stones. "You know what I mean. It was time for a change. Too much sameness clogs my energy."

"Typical Aquarius." Zora leaned over the countertop mirror and fluffed her halo of salt and pepper hair. "What happened to that nice young man in Eugene?"

No use pretending her aunt didn't know exactly what sent Gemma scurrying back to Trappers Cove, the seaside Washington town where she'd spent her childhood summers. "Caleb? He, uh—" *Dumped me. It hurts.* She cleared her throat to smooth the wobble from her voice. "He found someone new."

After three years of long-distance dating, punctuated by too-infrequent visits to Eugene, where Caleb taught at the University of Oregon, he'd let her down so tenderly there was nothing she could do but wish him well, then dash to her Jeep and steer for the coast. The ocean always gave her clarity, even in the depths of a blustery Pacific Northwest winter.

Straightening her shoulders, she pasted on a facsimile of a smile. "She seems nice, his new friend. I'm happy for him."

Zora gently pried the feather duster from her white-knuckled grip. "Darling, the world won't end if you admit you're hurting."

"Who says I'm hurting? I'm just ready for something new."

"Uh-huh," Zora deadpanned.

"Really, it's for the best," she insisted. "Every time I left Eugene, he sulked. When I came back, it was like starting from scratch. He said he loved me but—" She sighed and pinched the bridge of her nose. "Love isn't supposed to be this much work. It's supposed to click, to flow."

Zora arched one eyebrow. "And how has all this clicking and flowing worked out for you so far?"

Gemma squirmed under her aunt's sharp-eyed scrutiny. Delving into her feelings was about as appealing as disemboweling herself with a rusty knife. And as useful. *The heart is an internal organ for a reason. It's not meant to be displayed for all and sundry to dissect.*

But Zora had a point. Caleb's gentle dismissal knocked her way off balance. Once or twice during their relationship, she'd even felt the phrase "settle down" tickling the edges of her consciousness. Which was crazy for a free-spirited Aquarius like her. She was not the settling down type.

A month in Trappers Cove would help get her head on straight. And prepping for the big Portland expo gave her spinning thoughts a clear focus. Afterward, she'd return to Seattle, or Tacoma, or...

Zora rapped her knuckles on the glass countertop. "Earth to Gemma."

"Sorry. I was just cogitating."

"Always in your head. You should try thinking out loud sometime. Works great for me when I get stuck. I blather at Marquetta until a solution falls into place." She wound her arm around Gemma's waist. "I'm available for your blathering anytime the urge strikes you."

She heaved a lung-emptying sigh. "Maybe later. I need to sit with my thoughts for a while."

"Any plans for where you'll go next?"

She shrugged. "I'll know when the time is right to move on."

Zora cupped her cheek, forcing Gemma to meet her gaze. "At the risk of sounding like my stodgy brother-in-law, you're not a kid anymore. I hate to see you fritter away all this potential. Use that extraordinary intuition on yourself. You need a direction."

A prickly heaviness settled in Gemma's gut. "It's just—I'm interested in so many things, but so far, nothing has quite worked out the way I'd hoped."

Caleb said the same thing, more or less, when he asked her to return his apartment key. "You're a live wire, Gemma. Someday, when you find a focus for all that energy, you're going to make a real difference in the world. But I need a partner with more stability, someone I can build a home with, maybe start a family."

Clucking her tongue, Zora beckoned her toward the back of the shop. "Poor, conflicted vagabond. Let's see what the cards say."

"About what?" Gemma followed her behind the carved Balinese screen to the space where Zora practiced divination—mostly tarot cards, but she had other fortune-telling tools up her tie-dyed sleeve. From a drawer in the low table, Zora pulled a deck of tarot cards wrapped in red silk. "Just a simple three-card spread—you, your path, and your potential." She handed the cards to Gemma, who shuffled while searching for a question to focus the reading. Her frazzled mind yielded nothing useful.

Okay then, why not go with the mother of all questions?

"How can I be happy?" she asked aloud and flipped the top three cards onto the purple velvet tablecloth.

Zora pulled her reading glasses from her tunic pocket and set them on her button nose. "Oh my." She tapped the first card. "Seven of cups."

"I don't remember what that means." Despite her aunt's tutelage, Gemma had never really got a feel for the art of tarot. She had better luck with palmistry—at least that's what her friends said. Maybe they were just humoring her in exchange for hand massages.

"Quite simply, my dear, you're paralyzed by a plethora of possibilities. Constantly weighing all those options keeps you from moving forward." She patted Gemma's hand. "I know you hate to be tied down, but this could be your signal to get out of your head and make a choice based on the opportunities right in front of you."

Stay in Trappers Cove? As much as Gemma loved this funky little town, it was hard to imagine herself happy in such a small community. She got her juice from travelling—new faces, new possibilities, the ever-changing enticements of the open road, never staying in one place long enough to get bored.

Zora tapped the second card, a heart pierced with three swords. "That's an excellent sign. It's upside-down, see, so the swords fall out and healing begins. This is the card of silver linings, my dear. Help is on the way."

She tapped the third card. "Six of pentacles. See the scale he's holding? This represents a balance of giving and receiving. Be generous with what you have to give and be willing to accept help when it's offered." Zora quirked a crooked smile. "The balance can change at any time." She pushed her seat back. "Does that resonate with you?"

A bead of sweat trickled down Gemma's spine despite the winter chill.

"Here's the thing, Auntie—What do I have to give?"

Zora's soft hands enveloped hers. "So much, darling. You've always been a healer, the one your friends come to with their problems. Isn't that why you studied social work?"

Gemma snorted. "Until I dropped out. I had no idea how hard it is for social workers to make a real difference. They're so tangled up in red tape. I could never function within those confines."

"So, what's the wealth you're meant to share?"

"I'm good at helping people find their strengths." She huffed a bitter laugh. "Ironic, since I can't seem to pinpoint my own path." She ticked off on her fingers. "The literacy program in Seattle, the domestic violence shelter in Olympia, even the art therapy project in Eugene, they were all tangled up in rules and tight budgets. It's so frustrating when you're not allowed to do the right thing."

"So you came back here?"

She nodded. "Trappers Cove is so soothing. And I always feel at home in your shop."

Zora squeezed her hand. "You're always welcome, dear heart, and I'm grateful for your help."

Gemma traced the cards with her forefinger. "At least no one's throwing rules and regulations across your path."

Zora threw her head back and gave a hearty laugh. "Selling crystals and incense to tourists isn't exactly changing the world, darling."

"Don't belittle what you do, Auntie. All this—" She waved her hand, taking in the crystals, books, figurines, herbs, potions—"helps people see themselves and the world more clearly. Maybe this is what I'm meant to do too. I just need to find my angle."

"Nothing wrong with being a generalist, especially for someone like you who's fascinated by everything."

"Thanks, Auntie. I'll think on that." As usual, Zora's insight pierced Gemma's navel-gazing bullshit. She pushed her chair back. "Tell you what. Before we start planning for the Expo, let's smudge away stagnant energy from the old year. We need to clear new psychic pathways."

"Good idea, but I've already sold all my sage bundles." Zora glanced toward the door. "The herb guy is coming today."

"You sure? It's almost closing time."

Zora grinned. "Jesse's as dependable as the tides. He'll be here."

Chapter Two

♥

The brass doorbell tinkled as Jesse backed into Zora's shop cradling a carton of herbs the coastal wind seemed hell-bent on scattering. That happy jingle always brought a smile to his lips. Even though he didn't believe in all this woo-woo, new age bullshit, entering the hippie-dippy emporium was like getting a warm hug from a favorite auntie—one who smelled of patchouli and tea. Zora's place was a riot of color, full of funny, funky oddities like the fat, grinning Buddha perched on a burbling fountain beside the door. Or the dragon figurines glowering over their hoard of incense sticks. Or the display of tie-dyed socks.

His grin slipped when a stunning woman stepped from behind the wooden screen and froze, her plush mouth open, her eyes wide. A nagging sense of recognition tickled his memory—and his body. Where had he met her before? His skin prickled as he searched her face for clues, eerily certain they'd shared something momentous. Then it clicked.

The girl from the beach. She was back again—older now, but with the same tawny hair that fell in heavy waves, the same piercing eyes whose colors shifted with the light, the same tilt of her head like a clever bird who saw right through him. His heart gave a powerful thump, then kicked into overdrive.

Zora followed the beauty, her batik tunic billowing as she trotted toward him. "See, I told you," she called over her shoulder.

"Pardon?" He blinked rapidly, his feet rooted to the floor.

The old hippie mama beamed. "Jesse, you remember my niece Gemma, don't you?"

How could he ever forget?

Like the big, goofy teen he was when they first met, he shifted awkwardly from foot to foot. "You look different, Gemma. Your hair was longer last time, with purple tips, right? And you didn't have that squiggle tattoo on your hand."

She peered up at him through narrowed eyes. More green than blue today, they showed zero sign of recognition. That stung.

Stepping closer, she raised her slender hand and tapped the parallel zigzag lines. "Aquarius, my star sign. What's yours?"

Her nearness made his tongue thick and his brain sluggish. She smelled of lilacs and lemon verbena, like springtime on his gramps' farm. His farm now, though six months in, he still couldn't get used to thinking of it that way.

"Jesse's a Taurus." Zora patted his shoulder, took the delivery from his arms, and set it on the counter. "A classic example. Strong, steady, stubborn, and sensual."

His cheeks flushed hot enough to fry an egg.

"And he has the perfect Taurus name—del Toro."

Gemma tapped her pursed lips. "Why does that sound so familiar?" Just like all those years ago, her sexy pout spun his thoughts into a dizzy spiral of want and need.

Her ocean eyes crinkled. "Wait, didn't I see your name on the way to Westport? A farm stand or something?"

"Del Toro Botanicals," he croaked.

"Sounds like a cannabis farm." Her merry giggle tinkled like wind chimes.

He snorted. "I grow organic herbs—sage, oregano, dill, thyme—not weed."

"Organic herbs? That's so cool." He could practically see the cartoon hearts shooting from her eyes—but they were aimed at his carton of leaves and twigs, not at him.

"It's just a farm. You know, seeds, dirt, mud. Here." As he proffered a bundle of sage, his hand brushed hers. A zing danced up his arm. The sudden widening of her eyes proved she felt it too. Weird, considering he seldom drew much reaction from beautiful women. He'd never cultivated a confident swagger, and he had zero talent for small talk or witty flirtation. Just a dull homebody—according to Shauna, anyway.

The corners of Gemma's mouth ticked up. "You clean up nice, for a farmer." Snarky or flirtatious? Hard to tell.

"I scrape the mud off before coming to town."

"How's it going with the farm?" Zora asked.

"Still in the red but creeping slowly toward the black. Gramps' bookkeeping baffles me. It'll get better in spring when the farmers' markets start up again. Right now, my only customers are local restaurants, the organic food co-op, and you."

Zora squeezed his hand. "Frankie del Toro was a good man. I miss him."

"Me too." Six months after losing the man who was more father to him than his own dad ever was, he still expected to see Gramps striding through the greenhouse door or sipping coffee on the front porch of the rundown farmhouse he left to Jesse.

Gemma gazed up through misty eyes and grazed his arm with her fingertips. "You lost your grandfather? That must be so hard. I can tell you were close."

"How?"

"Our Gemma is quite intuitive." Zora edged away, a calculating smile on her apple dumpling face. "Let me go get my ledger." She ducked into the back of the shop, leaving them alone.

Her gaze darted to his, then away. She rubbed a leaf of sage between her fingers. "So soft and fuzzy." She closed her eyes, inhaled its scent, then rubbed it against her cheek. "Mmm." Her melodious hum struck a magic chord that made his dick jolt in his jeans. He tugged his jacket closed to cover the evidence.

"This is white sage, right? Do you grow other varieties?"

He gulped air and struck a casual pose, leaning on the counter. "I'm surprised you know the difference. Most woo-woo types don't."

Gemma's lip curled. "Some of us woo-woo types do our homework."

He raised his hands, palms out. "Hey, no offense intended. Your aunt's good people. What she does with the herbs is her business."

She scowled, a pretty flush painting her cheeks.

Great. Now he'd offended her. *Real smooth, dumbass.*

He cleared his throat. "Anyway, I've got blue sage, common garden sage, purple sage, pineapple sage…"

Zora returned with her ledger, her warm presence slicing the tension between them.

Gemma shot him a pointed glance. "Blue sage is good for dispelling negative energy." She addressed her aunt. "And pineapple sage eases anxiety. We should order some for smudge sticks and teas."

Zora scribbled in the ledger before pressing a check into his hand. "Speaking of—cup of tea, Jesse?"

"Thanks. Your tea is almost as good as my grandma's."

The old gal chuckled as she filled a paper cup from her antique samovar. "Someday I'll talk you into sharing her recipes. Quick tarot reading?"

Wincing, he rubbed the back of his neck. "You know I don't believe in that stuff."

Zora handed him the tea. "I bet you'd discover something unexpected about yourself."

"Yeah." Gemma added with a smirk. "A wise man keeps an open mind."

So much for impressing her. Ever since that long-ago summer, Gemma flitted through Trappers Cove like a butterfly every few years—a flash of delicate beauty that disappeared before he could approach her. As far as he knew, she'd never recognized him after that night on the beach.

"Good day, ladies." He tugged his cap low over his face and left the shop.

Before climbing into his truck, he paused to breathe in the sea air and check the rest of his deliveries. Here on Main Street, unimpeded by summer scents of caramel corn, corn dogs, and suntan lotion, the salty tang carried sweet and clear. A stiff wind had blown away yesterday's cloud cover. It was going to be a beautiful day. Too bad he'd be too busy to enjoy it. A walk on the beach would do him good.

But Casa Francesca had put in an urgent order for basil, thyme, and oregano. Trouble was, he was nearly out of Italian Oregano, so he'd brought Greek. Their flavor was similar, but Francesca was picky about her ingredients. Better call first before making the drive to her restaurant perched on a bluff north of town.

While on hold, his thoughts flicked back to Gemma. Once again, her beauty left him breathless. Dressed today in a long pine-green sweater, skin-tight jeans, and ankle boots, she looked like a forest enchantress from the fantasy books he loved as a kid.

Fixating on her was a waste of time. He had no place in his life for an airy-fairy hippie chick. If he took a chance on dating again, and that was a big if, he'd look for a woman who was down to earth, practical, like him. Too bad, though. Gemma's graceful movements and silky, deep voice forced an unwanted, primal reaction from his body. Yet another example of his lousy luck, always falling for women whose interest he couldn't hold.

He closed his eyes and tilted his face toward the sun until Francesca finally picked up.

Gemma stared through the shop's window at Jesse brooding beside his battered pickup. Where had she met him before? In a town as small as Trappers Cove, she must've run into him at some point. But her memory refused to yield up specifics, only a vague sense of knowing.

For a skeptical farmer, he packed a powerful punch. So damn good-looking, with a deep voice that vibrated her bones. With his brawny build and that curly forelock tumbling over his broad brow, he reminded her of a bull. Bull-headed, too. Experience had taught her it was best to avoid close-minded types like him. But oh, those brown eyes, warm as whiskey held up to firelight. How would that short, trim beard feel against her skin?

Her fingertips drifted to her throat and traced her collar bone.

"Cute, isn't he?"

She jolted at the sound of Zora's voice so close behind. *Sneaky old bird.*

Gemma tilted her chin toward the pretty farmer, resting against his truck with his handsome face turned to the sun. "Why does he work with you if he thinks what we do is some kind of scam?"

"He's a good man. Let him be who he is."

"But if he'd open his mind—"

Zora squeezed her arm. "Sometimes, darling, what people need most is to be accepted just as they are."

Gemma huffed a stray lock from her heated face. "And sometimes, people need a little push."

Outside, Jesse tucked his phone into his pocket and opened the door to his pickup.

A flash of inspiration brought a smile to her lips. "And I know just the way to do it." She hurried to intercept him.

"Hey, Jesse."

He turned toward her with a quizzical scowl.

"You know about the Esoteric Arts Expo in Portland next month?"

"Yeah. Got the extra herbs Zora ordered under a bank of grow-lights."

"You'll be there, right?"

His dark brows drew together. "At the expo? No. Why?"

Gemma grasped his arms, relishing the firm muscle through his thick woolen coat. "You've got an organic herb farm! You could offer teas, tinctures, potted plants. Give me a list of what you grow, and I'll write up their magical properties."

Jesse snorted, which only made him more bull-like. "Listen, I grow culinary herbs, stuff for tea and home remedies, not magic potions."

Yup, bull-headed to a fault. She forced her lips to unscowl. Being judgmental would get her nowhere with his type. He needed practical proof. "How could you ignore this huge market? The esoteric community is hungry for local products with integrity."

"My business is none of yours." With another sexy snort, he stepped closer and spread his stance, looming over her. "You ever actually worked the land, princess? It's not airy-fairy spirituality. It's heavy lifting and dirt under your nails." He held a broad palm before her face and wiggled his fingers. Immediately, her imagination zoomed to how those powerful hands would feel on her bare skin, their rough scrape raising goosebumps of pleasure. Would he be a forceful lover? Brutal, even? Or perhaps surprisingly tender?

She gave her head a little shake, took his hand, and inspected his palm. "Interesting Mount of Venus." She rubbed the base of his thumb. "Nice and fleshy."

She had his attention now. People loved being told about themselves. With narrowed eyes, he peered at the spot she was massaging. "Mount of Venus? What does that mean?"

"Fullness here shows you're passionate, sensual. And see this mark? Like a little X?"

He squinted, rumpling his eyebrows adorably.

"This means you have a lot of love to give." She was only quoting her library of palmistry books, but a skeptic like him would probably assume she was spouting pickup lines.

Instead of scoffing, he held her gaze for a long, heated moment. His nostrils flared, but whatever snarky comment he concocted remained behind his tightly pressed lips. His broad chest rose and fell.

Focus. Plan. Expo.

She forced her shoulders down. "So why not share some of that love with Zora and me? You help us with new products for the Esoteric Expo, and we'll help you with new customers for your herbs."

See? I can be practical and logical—just the way you like it, stubborn Taurus.

Still holding her gaze, Jesse flexed his jaw muscles as he thought it over.

Unwilling to break contact, Gemma continued to rub circles on his palm. "All I ask is a chance to peek inside." She meant his farm, of course. Ought to choose her phrasing more carefully. "Zora could really use some new products to draw in customers during the slow winter season." Giving into temptation, she sidled closer and inhaled his green, herbal scent. "Just an hour of your time? For Zora?"

With an exaggerated roll of his dark eyes, he huffed before giving her directions to his herb farm east of town.

"Excellent! I'll come by tomorrow morning. What's a good time?"

He smirked. "Six-thirty works for me."

Trying to scare me off. She squared her shoulders and served him a snarky grin of her own. "Great. See you then."

She sashayed back into the shop. Was it her imagination, or did he gun his truck's engine just for her? Battling his disbelief was going to be fun, and if she played her cards skillfully, she'd forge an alliance that benefited both him and her aunt. Maybe even earn some good-karma points to boost her next endeavor, whatever that might be.

And if the heat simmering in his dark eyes turned out to signify more than irritation?

Nope. Not so soon after the Caleb debacle. Hands off the hunky farmer.

Chapter Three

♥

Bumping along the dark rural road east of Trappers Cove, Gemma almost missed the turnoff to Jesse's herb farm. The faded wooden sign on the roadside hung crooked and half-hidden by a huckleberry bush. Honestly, it was like Jesse didn't even want customers to find him.

As she turned down the rutted gravel drive, her headlights illuminated fallow winter fields and neat rows of silvery-green lavender, blossomless this time of year. Slowing, she rolled down her window and inhaled their faint perfume, drifting on the damp, icy air.

Up ahead, the porch lamp shone from a single-story pale blue farmhouse flanked by stands of pine. Lights glowed inside and in the largest of three greenhouses to her right. Smaller outbuildings lay dark in the gray gloaming. She pulled her Jeep into an empty spot beside Jesse's truck and took a moment to breathe in the peaceful vibe, undisturbed except for crickets and a faint bang from inside the greenhouse. Seems Jesse was already at work.

What was his life like? Did he love the unyielding rhythm of farm life, or did he chafe under its demands? Being a Taurus, he'd probably blossom in a place like this where he could build a cozy home and sink deep roots. Must be nice, that feeling of belonging to a community—a vibe that eluded her except for during brief visits to Aunt Zora. She thought she'd found that kind of connection in Eugene, Oregon, but as soon as Caleb said goodbye, the artsy little city's welcoming aura evanesced.

Be here now.

Stepping out of her Jeep, she sucked in a deep breath of earth and green. No point in bemoaning the past when faced with such a beautiful present. Her footsteps crunched on the frosted grass as she made her way to the greenhouse, where a shadowy figure moved inside. The sign above the door, *Del Toro Botanicals*, needed new paint too. Her mind's eye illuminated an image of herself perched on a ladder as she refreshed that sign. Standing below, Jesse held a can of paint and smiled up at her...

Where the hell had that come from? Sure, the place needed sprucing up, but he hadn't asked for her help. Still, this was her chance to forge a connection to sustain Zora through the lean months until the tourists returned. The shop's bay window would be perfect for glass shelves holding plants—sage for purification, basil for attracting love and money, rosemary for memory, cinquefoil to invite blessings and favors. She chuckled. "Probably should have brought some of that today."

With luck, Jesse would have plenty of useful plants, since many cooking herbs also held spiritual powers. She rapped on the door and slid it open. The rush of fragrant, humid air almost knocked her off her feet.

"Wow. Concentrated oxygen." Grinning, she peeled off her winter coat and hat. Grow lights glowed over tables and ground-level planters filled with well-loved plants, some in blossom. This place held its own kind of magic. Despite his skepticism, the grumpy farmer was obviously a powerful green wizard.

"Jesse?" she called.

Clutching a hose, he rose from behind a table at the rear, and wow! A faded flannel shirt stretched tight over his broad shoulders, and worn jeans hugged his brawny thighs. Deep in her belly, something crackled and flashed like heat lightning.

Okay, so he's pretty. That's not why I'm here.

She forced a casual smile. "Good morning."

For a moment, he simply gaped at her, then scrubbed his free hand through his curly hair, mussing it adorably. "You came."

"You sound surprised."

He set down the hose and chuckled. "I didn't picture you as the type to get up with the roosters."

Gemma cocked a hip. "You don't think much of us woo-woo types, do you?" Honestly, getting up this early was no fun, but if you want to catch a farmer, you've got to move on his schedule. Not that she was trying to catch him, just seduce him. Into a business deal.

Focus, Gemma.

She needed to keep her eyes on the prize, not on Jesse's hunky bod and teasing grin.

"This is a special place. I can sense all the love you put into these plants. Excellent vibes. Lots of potential for healing."

"You make it sound like some kind of temple." He lifted a narrow trowel. "It's just a greenhouse."

"Oh, it's so much more than that." She sauntered toward him, taking a zig-zag path between the planters as she caressed the tender leaves and inhaling their fragrance.

"You're right, I guess." Bending over a table, he prodded the soil. "The farm is all I have left of my grandparents. They loved this place. Working here makes me feel close to them."

Funny that he didn't mention his parents. Sore subject?

Hunched over, he talked to the plants as much as to her. "Gran and Gramps started this place during the seventies when Trappers Cove was a hippie mecca. If it weren't for farmers' markets and farm-to-table restaurants, I'd have had to shut down. Nowadays, most people buy their plants from big-box stores. They don't care about quality, just price."

The gentle way he handled the delicate lives in his care sent a whisper of longing through her. Would he touch a lover with the same tenderness?

Jesse's defensive gruffness melted away when talking about his little green babies. She'd come armed against his snark, but his unexpected reverence caught her defenseless.

It would be damned easy to make a fool of herself over this sweet man.

"You really love this place." She stepped to his side. "Not only the farm, but the town. It shines through in your voice, your eyes…"

He straightened and faced her. "Trappers Cove is home, and this farm is my little piece of it. When it thrives, I thrive." His gaze softened. "How about you?"

"I always love coming back to TC, but I love a lot of places." His probing gaze unnerved her, so she turned away and traced the delicate serrated leaves of a vervain plant. "Trappers Cove will always be one of my home bases."

He quirked an eyebrow. "How many home bases do you have?"

Her stomach tightened—which was dumb. Why should she feel so defensive? Lots of people prefer to roam about rather than settle in one place.

Raising her chin, she ticked off on her fingers. "There's Olympia, where I grew up. And Seattle, where I went to college." No need to mention the part where she dropped out. "There's Tacoma, where I worked at a domestic violence shelter, and Leavenworth, where my friend runs a spa." She almost mentioned Eugene, Oregon, but would she ever feel comfortable returning there? "I guess you could say I have an orbit, like a comet."

Jesse snorted.

Indignant, she glared up at him. "What's that's about?"

"Pretty hard to grow if you're afraid to sink roots."

Her spine stiffened. "Who says I'm afraid? Maybe people who stay put all the time are terrified to stretch their wings and fly."

Jesse didn't flinch. "I don't have wings, princess. I'm just a man, walking on the ground." He patted a planter box. "This is my home. I like it here."

Argh! His placid expression made her want to poke him harder. "Don't you crave a change of scenery sometimes?"

"Sure, travel's nice, but this place takes my constant attention." Moving to the translucent wall, he fiddled with a timer attached to a spigot.

She heard Zora's voice urging her to let Jesse be, but she couldn't help herself. "You could hire helpers."

He snorted again. "Gotta start earning a profit first. Besides, I can't stand to be away for long. I'd worry too much." He lifted one shoulder. "Gramps always said it takes all kinds to make the world go 'round. Your type will never understand my type, I guess."

His comment stung like nettles. Had she been unfair to Jesse? She'd never get what she wanted by antagonizing him.

She blew out a breath and turned back to the plants. "Okay if I take some photos to help me remember which herbs we can use for Zora's shop?"

"Be my guest. All the herbs are in this greenhouse. The others hold ornamental plants and spring bulbs."

Forcing her gaze away from the frustrating farmer, she wandered the gravel aisles between planters, snapping photos and taking notes. After a few silent minutes, her restraint crumbled.

"Vervain protects against the evil eye, you know."

"Uh huh," he intoned in a flat voice.

"And catnip aids divination."

"You don't say."

So much for conversation. Moving farther away, she snuck glances at him as he worked. When he bent over a low planter, his shirt rode up, baring a swath of muscular back. She nearly swooned.

Get ahold of yourself. This guy isn't for you. He'd basically warned her off, anyway, and as enchanting as this place was, she could never be happy rooting herself to one spot, even one as dear to her as Trappers Cove. If she wanted another man—which, at the moment, she did not, thank you very much—she'd find a free spirit like herself, not a stodgy farmer.

Backing up to take a photo, she bonked into a solid wall of muscly male, then sprang back like a startled cat. "Sorry. Clumsy of me."

"My fault." He pulled a bandana from his shirt pocket and wiped his face and—*oh Goddess!*—rolled up his sleeves to display muscular forearms dusted with dark hair.

Her tongue thickened in her mouth.

Jesse inclined his head. "Let me show you the mint bed. You said Zora wanted to make tea." He led her to a low bed brimming with different varieties.

"This one's my favorite. Chocolate mint." He plucked a sprig and held it to her nose. As she took it, their hands brushed, and her whole body tingled in response. His deep, rumbly voice continued, but his words got lost in the horny haze enveloping her.

"Gemma?" He gently squeezed her shoulder. "You okay?"

"Fine. Fine. I'm fine." She giggled nervously. "Just a little off balance. Guess I should've eaten something before coming out here."

The faintest hint of a smile played across his lips. "Come into the house. I got you up this early. Least I can do is give you breakfast."

"No, no, I—"

"Listen." His grin widened. "I need a break too. I've got zucchini muffins and my grandma's special winter tea. It'll warm you right up."

Heart skittering, she followed him down the gravel path and up the porch steps into a cozy kitchen. While he filled the electric kettle and slid muffins into the toaster oven, she took in her surroundings. Not stodgy at all. Homey and traditional, for sure, but with personality and attention to comfort. The tabletop was cut from a single slab of wood, its natural grain and rough edges showing the spirit of the tree that birthed it. Heavy, rustic chairs were topped with plush cushions. A pellet stove in the corner radiated warmth. In the center of the table, a hand-thrown pottery vase held dried flowers and herbs. Every detail blended to weave a relaxing, welcoming space.

He waved toward the table. "Sit. Make yourself comfortable."

Watching him work at the rough-hewn wooden counter, she was struck with another vision—Jesse bending her over that same counter in a deep kiss, his strong hands tunneling under her clothes, grasping, kneading, teasing her to peak after peak of pleasure...

"Goddess help me," she muttered, fanning herself. Must be low blood sugar.

He set a pottery mug of steaming tea before her. His brow rumpled. "You okay?"

"Yeah. Sure." She grinned up at him, probably looking a bit rabid.

He slid a plate of muffins toward her, along with a homespun cloth napkin. "Grandma's recipe—nothing fancy. You know how it is with summer zucchini—you always harvest more than you can use."

She inhaled the sweet scent of nutmeg, cloves, and cinnamon, then took a bite. "Delicious." They chewed in silence for a moment, Jesse's eyes never leaving her face. Was he afraid she was going to pass out in his kitchen? One more sexy vision, and she just might.

She cleared her throat. "Well, thanks for letting me look around your greenhouse. All that healthy oxygen must've stimulated my brain. I've got all kinds of cool ideas cooking."

"Do tell." He quirked a dangerously dazzling smile.

"For the expo, I mean, and for Zora's shop. She's been like a mother to me—more than my own mom, to tell you the truth."

"Yeah." He wiped crumbs from his lips, leaving a few clinging to his trim beard. "Zora is good people."

"Even though she's woo-woo?"

He leaned onto his elbows and fixed her with an intense gaze that sent tingles down her spine. "Listen, if I gave you the impression I don't respect your aunt, I apologize. That's not true at all. She's a great lady, and in her own way, she helps people."

"Oh really? How?"

"She makes you think, and she's gentle about it. It's easy to get stuck in your own thought patterns. A fresh point of view never hurts, even if it comes from a deck of tarot cards or, you know, palmistry." His smile held a teasing edge.

She scooted her chair closer. "Mr. Skeptic wants to learn about his lines? How about I give you a reading? Call it my thank-you for breakfast."

With an adorable, bashful grin, he extended his palm.

"You're a lefty, yes?" She grasped his other hand and opened it. "Your non-dominant hand shows your natural tendencies." She traced the arc around his thumb. "Your life line is deep and clear."

"That's good, right?"

She nodded. "Means you enjoy life. You have courage and plenty of energy. But see this break here?"

Squinting, he peered at the spot.

"This shows a tendency to spend more time thinking than acting. Don't be afraid to take risks."

"Hmmph. On new ventures with a certain woo-woo shop, for example?"

"Hey, I didn't etch these lines." She shot him a snarky smile. "Now this head line is typical of a Taurus."

He huffed. "No one likes being told they're typical."

"You want flattery or information?"

He rolled his eyes and huffed a sigh. "Go ahead."

"It's actually a good sign, by the way. The length of your head line means you're perceptive and fair. You're opinionated, but you enjoy learning new things. Teaching would be a good job for you."

"Me? In a classroom full of kids? No thanks."

"Not all teachers work in classrooms, or even in schools." Easy to imagine him using his beautiful greenhouses to teach about herbalism, but let him figure that one out on his own. "Palmistry isn't about foretelling the future, it's about knowing yourself so you can make better choices."

"Fair enough. What about, um, the other line?"

Mr. Grumpy Bull wanted to know about his love life? Another good sign. With her fingertip, she traced the crease beneath his fingers. "The heart line isn't only about romance, it's about your feelings for all the important people in your life—friends, family, lovers. Yours is deeply etched. You care a lot about home and family."

He huffed through his nose. "Already told you that."

"Uh-huh. Your love for your family shows in all the care you put into making your home and farm beautiful, comfortable, and welcoming."

Who'd have thought such a big, sullen bull would blush so prettily? She tamped down her urge to tease, suspecting that Jesse rarely opened himself to strangers like this.

"And your heart line extends all the way to your index finger. That means you're a romantic, very protective and nurturing."

His gaze shifted away. "Fat lot of good that does me," he grumbled.

"Care to elaborate?"

"No." Setting his lips in a firm line, he clenched his hand. "Thanks for the reading."

Touched a nerve, did I?

"Anytime." She patted his knuckles.

Still grumbling, he collected their empty plates. "You're probably spinning bullshit so you can have your way with my plants."

She shot to her feet. "Now just a goddamn minute. I didn't come here to be insulted. I came to help you. And Zora, someone you claim to care about."

He glared at his boots, his jaw working.

Clearly her so-called intuition was on the fritz today. She'd read him as a secret softy, but he was just another prickly, hostile dude-bro, out of touch with all his feelings except anger. The electricity she sensed between them was merely wishful thinking, triggered by her bruised ego.

Finally, he took a halting step toward her, his gaze lowered. "Look, I'm sorry. You did nothing to deserve that."

She crossed her arms. "Correct. I didn't."

"I apologize." He pronounced the words like he was swallowing bitter medicine. "And I do want to hear your plans. For my plants, I mean."

He was drawing a line—business connection, maybe. Personal connection, a firm no.

She sucked in a huge breath and tried to exhale the tightness from her chest. "Here's what I was thinking—custom tea blends for sweet dreams, mental clarity, insight, calm in times of stress, opening the heart to new love..."

His chuckle rang as dry as burnt toast. "That's a lot to ask from a cup of tea."

She lifted her chin. "Herbs have proven properties going back to ancient medicine systems. A botanist like you should know that."

Again, his gaze dropped to the floor. "Told you, I'm just a farmer."

Her patience snapped. She jabbed her finger into his broad chest. "Well, open your mind, farmer boy. You'd find lots of new customers if you'd get your head out of your—" Catching herself just in time, she sucked in a breath and raised her palms. "Sorry. I shouldn't yell at you after you let me into your inner sanctum."

Shaking his head, Jesse shrank back. "It's a greenhouse, Gemma."

She softened her tone and laid her hand on his forearm. "Yeah, but this place holds your heart. I'm honored you invited me in." She moved to the front door and shrugged into her coat. "I'll send you a list of herbs we'd like to buy. Could we get some potted plants too? I'd like to try making fairy gardens."

His forehead rumpled. "Do what now?"

Why did he have to be so damn cute?

"You know, little terrariums in a dish, with aromatic plants and figurines. Big sellers at the farmers' markets in Eugene and Portland.

Zora has a ton of tiny tchotchkes we could use. Buddha meditating under the sage tree, Ganesha dancing in the creeping thyme…"

At last, his stiff posture relaxed. "Sounds cute. Okay. As long as you're not using my plants to hex anyone, I'm game."

She held up three fingers in a Scout's Honor gesture. "No hexing, only healing." She reached for the doorknob.

His big hand fell onto her shoulder. "Listen, Gemma, I'm sorry for sounding disrespectful. You and Zora aren't hurting anyone, and if you can help her business and mine, well, I'm grateful."

"From skepticism to gratitude. That's quite a leap in just one morning."

Their eyes met and held. Maybe it was the welcoming spirit of his home, maybe the phase of the moon, but she found herself gripping his shirt, rising on tiptoe, and aiming a smooch at his cheek. Startled, he jerked so her kiss landed at the corner of his mouth. His wide, soft lips parted on a sharp inhalation. They both staggered back.

Her face roasting, she clutched her coat over her chest. "Okay then, I'll get to work. On the, uh, plants." She backed through the door, heart fluttering like a hummingbird.

Jesse followed, his steps jerky. He rubbed the back of his neck. "Say, you want to have dinner sometime?"

"Sometime?"

"Like, maybe Friday? Farmer friend of mine is delivering some organic lamb. I was gonna make stew."

Knocked completely sideways by this turn of events, she gawked like an idiot.

He grinned and shrugged. "I promise, it's really good. Or are you a vegetarian? I could make something else."

The menu wasn't the problem, her bruised heart was, and the fact that she'd be leaving Trappers Cove in a month or two. But Zora had assured her Jesse was a good man, and she wouldn't be in town long enough to fall in love, so... "Okay. Why not? I'd love to taste your cooking." *And other things.*

His brilliant grin fried her brain. Time to go. "I'll see you Friday."

She spun and returned to her Jeep on wobbly legs. What an emotional rollercoaster! As she drove back to town, the coastal fog swirling around her aged Jeep, she debated with herself—was dinner with Jesse a harmless indulgence or a terrible mistake?

Chapter Four

♥

The winter sun hung low in the sky when Jesse spotted Ryan's shiny blue Ram pickup bumping up the gravel road. That behemoth was his best friend's pride and joy. No doubt, he'd stop by a carwash to clean off the dust on his way back to his brew pub on Main Street.

Ryan was a weird contradiction. He dressed impeccably to impress his customersi but loved to sink his hands into the dirt. His apartment above the Salty Dog Brewery and Saloon only offered a tiny balcony, so he regularly visited Jesse's farm for a little therapeutic gardening. Said it helped him think.

Ryan switched off his headlights, hopped down from his truck, and flashed a shit-eating grin. "So, did she show?"

"Come again?"

"The girl, dumbass. The hippie hottie. Did you scare her off?"

"Not quite." Jesse wiped his dirt-smeared hands on his jeans. "She's coming over for dinner on Friday."

"Attaboy." Ryan pounded Jesse's back. "Way to get back on the horse."

His jaw tightened. "I told you, I'm over Shauna."

"Uh-huh. Keep tellin' yourself that."

Jesse and Shauna had dated for the past two years or so. A teacher at the elementary school, she was one of the few younger residents besides Jesse and Ryan who grew up in Trappers Cove and actually stuck around. Unlike most of their classmates, who left for wider pastures, Shauna had seemed to love TC as much as he did, and until recently, he really thought she was the one. Not that he burned for her or any such nonsense, but they fit comfortably together to the point where he'd started envisioning a family of his own in this old farmstead.

But Shauna neglected to tell him she'd applied for a job in Seattle, and as soon as she got an offer, she booked it out of Trappers Cove without a backward glance. The memory of her parting words still stung.

"I just feel like what we had has run its course. You're a great guy, Jesse, but we each want a different kind of life. I need more than this." Her limp wave had taken in all he held dear—the house, the farm, the town.

He picked up a stone and chucked it across the field of sage, thyme, and rosemary, watching it sail end over end into the sunset. "Shauna wasn't the one for me. Neither is Gemma, most likely."

"Why'd you ask her out then?" Ryan dragged his ostrich-skin boot through the dust, dislodged a stone, and spun it expertly toward the horizon.

"Dunno." He bent to find another projectile. "There's something about her that's just—exciting, I guess. But she's so freakin' woo-woo. Asked my star sign, for God's sake."

"And she comes and goes, right? Probably not the best choice for a homebody like you. You tend to stay in your comfort zone."

Jesse executed a slow turn, drinking in the familiar beauty of his homestead. The greenhouses glowed in the gathering twilight.

Heather bloomed in flower boxes on the porch railing, and Gramps' well-loved rocking chair waited for Jesse's evening drink and contemplation. He cherished this place, and maintaining it took his full attention. So why were stupid thoughts of a future with Gemma tickling his imagination? He hadn't even kissed the woman—at least, not properly.

But he really wanted to.

Staring into the distance, Ryan rubbed his chin. "On the other hand—"

With Ryan, there was always an "on the other hand."

"How many available women are you gonna meet in Trappers Cove in winter? Most of the locals are paired up, and the single ones don't stay." His smile slipped sideways. "Like Reese." A massage therapist at the Sea Queen Spa, she'd kept Ryan enchanted with her flirty glances and magic hands—until she got a better offer from a spa in Bellevue and flew the coop.

Jesse picked up another stone, flat and smooth, and pitched it toward the tree line. "Yeah, the good ones always leave."

Ryan bumped Jesse's shoulder with his own. "Sorry, man. You still hurting?"

He heaved a sigh that emptied his lungs. Ryan had an uncanny way of teasing the truth past his defenses. It hurt sometimes, but he always felt better afterward. "If I'm honest with myself, I don't miss Shauna as much as I miss the future I imagined for us. That's what I get for assuming."

"Well, good on you for asking out the hippie chick. You need to exercise your dating muscles." He gave Jesse's arm an affectionate punch. "You used to be charming, you know."

Jesse chuckled. "Yeah, I just need practice, right?" But deep down, he knew he was playing with fire. Gemma was not the kind of woman you dabble with and then forget. Though she'd left his place early this morning, the residual glow still clung. If he was woo-woo like her, he'd call it a good vibe, one he yearned to explore.

"Gemma's special, for sure." He couldn't help smiling at the memory of her teasing, the way she breathed in the beauty of the greenhouse and exhaled—what? Possibility? Optimism? "She's one of those women where, once you look at her, really look at her, you can't look away."

Ryan clapped Jesse's shoulder. "My friend, sounds like you've got a bad case of insta-lust."

"Insta what now?"

"Like in those romance books Daphne's always pushing." Ryan's older sister ran the town's bookshop, catering to tourists and locals alike.

Jesse chuckled. "Maybe I better start reading those."

Chapter Five

♥

Friday evening, Gemma paused on Jesse's front porch. Host gift? Check. Wine? Check. Hole-free lingerie and condoms, just in case? Check.

What she really ought to check was her expectations. Hard to imagine a worse match for her free-spirited self than taciturn, close-minded Jesse Del Toro. And yet, her intuition kept nudging her toward him. Okay, less a nudge and more of a shove. She'd learned the painful way that ignoring these messages was a bad idea. So she sucked in a deep breath, squared her shoulders, and reached for the doorbell.

The door opened before she could ring, revealing Jesse's teasing grin. "Wondered how long you were gonna stand out there. Saying some kind of magic spell?"

"Maybe." Easier to tease back than admit her nervous dithering. "You look nice."

Awkward thing to say to a guy, perhaps, but wow. His soft, chambray shirt molded to his broad shoulders and muscular chest, with the top buttons undone to reveal a shadow of dark hair below his collar bones. Her fingers twitched with the urge to touch him there—and to follow the firm curves of his arms, to tug that shirt free from his belt and—

"Here." She pulled a polished, blue-black stone from her pocket. "From Zora's collection. Black tourmaline. Good for masculine energy." She dropped it into his palm. "Not that you need any help in that area." *Is my face as red as it feels?* "It also repels negativity and helps ward off your fears."

He glanced from the stone to her face, brows contracted. "So you know exactly which rock I need to repair my aura? Or chakras? Or whatever?"

She hadn't considered the possibility he'd be insulted by her gift. Way to make sure their first date was their last.

"No, of course not. I mean, I hardly know you, Jesse. But I'd like to."

Yowza. She also hadn't counted on this awkward truth avalanche.

"Hmmph." Lips scrunched to the side, he turned the stone over and over with long, nimble fingers. "So you give me a magic rock to persuade me to go into business with you and Zora?"

She lifted her chin in an attempt to recapture a little dignity. "No. I was reorganizing Zora's crystal display, and this one felt right for you."

Still silent, he raised an eyebrow.

She sighed. "I wouldn't expect you to understand."

The corners of his mouth hitched upward. "Well, I don't, but I appreciate the thoughtful gesture." He rubbed the tourmaline with his thumb, then slipped it into his front jeans pocket. "It'll make a good worry stone." His grin heated a few degrees. "Or should I not keep it so close to my, erm, masculine energy?"

Heat flooded her face.

Inching closer, he touched her cheek with his fingertip. "You're pretty in pink."

"Ha ha." She lifted her other offering from her bag. "Aunt Marquetta's blackberry wine."

Jesse's expression softened as he took the bottle. "My gramps used to make this stuff."

Well, at least one gift landed.

"Come on in." With his hand on the small of her back, he led her into the kitchen where they'd shared coffee last week. Tonight, the antique dining hutch and sideboard flickered with tea candles in mason jars, old-school jelly jars, and cut-glass tumblers. In the center of the table, a bouquet of fragrant, fresh herbs. She leaned over it to inhale their scent, then peeked from behind her curtain of hair at the enticing shift of Jesse's muscles as he moved around the room. His hips swayed ever so slightly to the soft, bluesy guitar wafting from a speaker on the counter.

She sighed, mesmerized by the sight of this big, burly bull-man in his home element. All too soon, he hefted an enamel Dutch oven and carried it to the table. "Let's eat."

With a dented ladle, he filled rustic pottery bowls with hearty lamb stew. "Organically raised meat from my buddy's farm."

Gemma braced herself for disappointment. Her taste ran more toward spicy dishes, exotic ingredients, bold combinations. But the stew was flavored with herbs from his greenhouse, ditto the salad, and Jesse's homemade bread was flecked with fresh dill. These extra touches added surprising depth to the simple meal.

"Everything's delicious," she told him with complete honesty.

Dinner was quieter than she'd expected, a circumstance that normally made Gemma uncomfortable and self-conscious. But Jesse's sort of quiet was soothing, and the open, attentive way he watched her did funny things to her core—not simply lust, though there certainly was that. This feeling of ease with a near-stranger scared her a little, because how could something so easy possibly last? Good thing she wasn't staying long in Trappers Cove. Jesse could tie a major knot in her plans.

"Got room for dessert?" he asked as he pushed his chair back. "I made it with you in mind."

She pointed to her chest.

"Yes, you." He chuckled.

"Wow. No one's ever dedicated a dessert to me before. Guess I've gotta try it."

His sweet smile flattened. "I mean, you don't have to if you don't want to."

She popped from her chair. "No, I do!" *And why has my voice gone all squeaky?* "I'd love to see what kind of dessert reminds you of me."

"Cool." His smile returned. "Want to eat outside? I'll light the fire pit."

Truth be told, she was more in the mood for a post-meal cuddle on his couch. When she hesitated, he added, "It's propane. No smoke."

"Sure, okay. Sounds like fun." She did her best to inject enthusiasm into her voice.

"Great." His grin widened. "Give me a minute."

Preparations accomplished, he returned to the kitchen and beckoned her outside.

Her breath puffed into the clear, cold night air. Stars twinkled in a crystalline sky. All around the little farmhouse, towering pines swayed like silent sentinels. Between the porch and the greenhouse, a firepit-table thingy crackled merrily beside an oversized Adirondack chair for two, decked with fluffy sheepskin fleeces and colorful woolen blankets. On the table's rim sat two earthenware mugs, a thermos, and a covered cake plate.

Indoors or outdoors, Jesse Del Toro had an amazing eye for detail.

While she gawked, he pulled back the blanket, sat, and patted the seat beside him. "I promise not to bite unless you ask me to."

That smile is absolutely lethal. With a gulp, she settled against him and wiggled her butt into the cushy fleece. "This is perfect, Jesse."

His shoulder pressed against hers as he covered their laps with a blanket, layered another one on top, then lifted the dome on the cake plate. The way he nibbled his plump lower lip made her want to help him with that task—the lip nibbling, not the cake serving.

"I candied these lilacs last spring." He slid a slice of glazed yellow Bundt cake topped with sparkly purple gems onto her plate.

She waited until he served himself before taking a bite. The lemon flavor hit the perfect sweet/tart note, and the candied blossoms lent a complex floral counterpoint.

"Incredible." She licked her fork, then her lips. "This cake reminds you of me?"

His thick lashes lowered. "Yeah. I guess you inspired me."

Hard to imagine a greater compliment. "Care to explain?" She elbowed him. "Are you telling me I'm tart?"

"Sometimes." He returned her nudge, then kept her waiting as he chewed. Devil, he enjoyed keeping her in suspense.

"Jesse, don't tease." She shoved him harder, a pointless gesture, since she could no more move his strong, solid body than she could budge a bull.

"Says the woman who teases me about being a fuddy-duddy."

"I never called you a—"

"Potato, potahto." He stared her down for a tense moment, then cracked a grin and took another bite.

This time, she poked him with her fork.

"Okay, okay." He forked up another morsel and held it under her nose. "This reminds me of your perfume—lilacs and something lemony."

"Lemon verbena." Not only had he noticed the details of the scent she mixed from essential oils, but he'd also created an edible tribute. Had any past lover paid such careful attention?

Tears prickled her eyes—and no smoke to blame them on. *Oh, what the hell.* Just this once, she wouldn't hide her emotional reaction, even if it was sappy.

"Jesse." She twined her fingers through his. "I don't think I've ever been more flattered. Thank you."

Firelight flickered in his dark irises. Breathless, she silently prayed for the kiss she craved. He licked his lips, a slow, sensual gesture. His gaze slid away. "Tea?"

Well, shit. Wrong again.

"Sure." She forced a cheerful tone.

He unscrewed the thermos's lid and poured a stream of amber liquid into her mug. "My grandmother's sweet dreams tea. Gran was kind of a hippie. Believed in the old home remedies."

"Like me?"

Jesse huffed a laugh as he filled his own cup. "Forgive me if I have a hard time comparing you to my grandma."

She sipped, hiding her disappointed pout behind her oversize mug. "Lemme guess—she was steady, like you. Not like me, bouncing from place to place."

With a gentle touch, Jesse removed the mug from her fingers and set it on the table's rim. He traced the curve of her cheek with his callused fingertip, igniting shivers of pleasure.

"Gran was a wonderful woman, wise and kind. That part is like you. But she was, well, my grandma. Soft, comfortable." Through the blanket, he rubbed her thigh in slow, measured strokes. "And you—" A low hum rumbled in his chest as his gaze danced over her face, her body. "You're more like the fire—leaping and dancing, bright sparks that burn themselves into my memory and then disappear. When I close my eyes, I can still see them. Just like I see you long after you leave—in the greenhouse, In my kitchen, in my dreams." As he spoke, he moved closer until his lips hovered mere inches from hers.

Spellbound, she waited as Jesse feathered his fingers through her hair, over her jaw, his dark eyes sparkling.

Burning desire bulldozed the last of her patience. With a moan, she wound her arms around his neck and pulled him in to claim what she needed.

But the stubborn bull reared back with a teasing smile. "Easy. I don't want to rush this." He nudged her woolen scarf aside and kissed the sensitive skin below her ear. Sparks danced from the tender press of his lips to the tips of her toes.

"Jesse, we don't have much time together." His curly hair was so soft beneath her fingers.

He chuckled. "I'll make it worth the wait, I promise."

With a groan, she let her head loll back and submitted to his un-hurried exploration. This was a new sensation for a woman used to grabbing what she wanted. Nerves as taut as violin strings, breath shallow, she relished each thrill until Jesse mercifully pressed his warm, soft lips to hers.

The moan rumbling through his broad chest melted her bones. He pulled back far enough to pierce her with his gaze. "You're going to break my heart, aren't you?"

"Not necessarily." She stroked his beard, scratchy-soft beneath her palms. More likely, she'd fall hard for this surprising, stunning man who'd find out soon enough how hard she was to love. But for now, she'd accept the pleasure he offered.

She toyed with the silky curls at his nape as he pressed kisses to her forehead, cheeks, and throat before returning to her hungry mouth. His tongue teased her lips apart and entered, all velvet seduction, a slow tango that built higher and higher. She arched toward him, craving more contact. With a low laugh, he tugged the blankets up to cover them both, unfastened her jacket, and slid his hands over her sides, his thumbs teasing the outer curve of her breasts.

It was like being a desperately horny teen again, making out in the bleachers at a football game, but hotter because Jesse knew how to prolong each caress, bringing her to dizzying heights of arousal.

"Please," she moaned into his hair as he traced her collar bones with his tongue.

"Please what, beauty?"

"Touch me." She arched her breasts toward him, but his hands slid around her back, massaging her gently.

"I am touching you."

Such a damn tease. He was going to make her ask for what she wanted. She grasped one elusive wrist and brought his hand to her breast. "No, here."

With a devilish laugh, he pressed his forehead to hers. "Like this?" He kept his touch light, the barest brush over her sweater. Her nerves screamed.

"More. I need to feel your hands on my skin."

"Mmm." At last, his fingers slid beneath her sweater, the combination of rough callus and gentle strength driving her higher. And when those powerful hands tugged her bra down to roll and pinch her nipples, she jolted against him. A few more minutes of this and she'd come without even feeling his touch on her core.

She threw her leg over him and ground against his brawny thigh, seeking release.

Her phone shrilled. Zora's ringtone.

"Not now, Auntie," she groaned.

Jesse lifted her sweater and licked her breast, his tongue circling closer and closer to her aching nipple.

The phone rang again, Marquetta's ringtone this time.

"No, no, no," she whimpered. "Let me have this moment."

An unfamiliar ringtone sounded. With a sigh, Jesse withdrew and pulled his phone from his jacket pocket. "Uh-oh." He held up the screen. "Zora's number. You better take this." He hit Speaker.

Marquetta's voice rang out, tense and tight. "Thank God. We're on our way to the E.R. Zora was working late at the shop. She got dizzy and fell. Hit her head on that damn giant geode by the door. Blood everywhere."

"I'm on my way." Heart hammering, Gemma fumbled with her clothing.

"I'll drive you." Jesse pocketed his phone and turned off the firepit.

"No, you don't need to—"

"I said, I'm driving." Jaw tight, nostrils flared, he'd never looked more like his namesake beast as he yanked her to her feet and boosted her into his pickup.

"Bull-headed farmer," she muttered as he spun out, spraying gravel.

"When I have to be. You're too upset to drive." He stomped the accelerator as soon as they hit the road.

Shivering, Gemma huddled in her seat. "Goddess, please let her be okay." What would she do without her beloved auntie?

Jesse's big hand clasped her knee. "She will be. Zora is strong, like her niece."

Wishing she could believe him, she leaned onto his shoulder as they sped toward town.

Chapter Six

❤

By the time Jesse pulled into the parking lot of Trappers Cove's small community hospital, Gemma's wrenching sobs had quieted, but she continued to clutch his knee in a white-knuckled grip. What could he possibly do or say to comfort her? Despite their interrupted intimacy, he hardly knew her—her spicy wit, her teasing smile, yes, and her silken skin, and sea-bright eyes, but heart remained a mystery.

He switched off the ignition and pulled her hand into his. "Whatever we find in there, we'll handle it together, okay? Just tell me what you need."

She gazed at him with red, puffy eyes. "Why are you being so nice to me?"

He chuckled. "If you don't know the answer to that question, I need to work on my technique."

When she gave him a quizzical head tilt, he added, "I like you, Gemma. A lot. And I'm fond of Zora and Marquetta too." He pulled her hand to his lips and kissed it. "Now, let's go see what needs to be done."

Perhaps it was a shitty, selfish thought, but he liked the way she leaned on him as they hurried to the ER.

A kindly nurse directed them down a long hallway to a narrow room where Zora lay in bed, sallow and small against the pillows, a large gauze bandage on her forehead, wires trailing from her body to a bank of monitors. A steady beep, beep, beep punctuated her whispered conversation with Marquetta, who clutched her wife's hand.

"Auntie," Gemma sobbed and bolted to join them. She gave Zora a careful hug and Marquetta a tight, teary one.

Marquetta shot him a baleful glance. "Something's wrong with her heart's rhythm. They're shipping her to Aberdeen for testing."

"How long will that take?"

The tremor in Gemma's voice made him yearn to hold her close, but he restrained himself, unsure if she'd welcome the gesture.

Zora shook her head. "Doc says I need bed rest and zero stress. Maybe it's time to give up the shop."

"Babe, no." Marquetta sank onto the bed's edge. "You put so much heart and soul into renovating the place."

"Then I'll close it until I'm better." Zora crossed her arms and winced as her hospital wristband caught on a monitor wire.

"You're running on a thin margin as it is," her wife countered. "I'll take a leave of absence from the library."

"Don't be ridiculous. Who's gonna keep the doors open, the volunteers?"

Gemma lifted her chin. "I'll run the shop, Auntie. You can supervise from your bed. We'll FaceTime."

Zora gentled her tone. "Darling, you're one of the most creative, intuitive people I've ever met, but you don't know diddly squat about running a business. You never stay put long enough to learn the boring details."

He couldn't bear another minute of this stubborn squabbling. Three of his favorite people in Trappers Cove were in distress. He straightened and moved to Gemma's side. "I'll help."

Marquetta's voice wobbled. "You kids would do that for us?"

Placing her hand over his heart, Gemma gazed up at him, her tear-bright eyes enormous. Something passed between them in that moment—something big and powerful that filled his chest with warmth and lifted his feet a hair's breadth off the ground.

"Of course we will," she told the two older women. "You rest up, Auntie Z. Let Marquetta take care of you."

Zora and Marquetta exchanged a wary glance. Stubborn old birds.

He leaned down and took Zora's hand, careful not to disturb her IV port. "Come on, let Gemma manage the customers. She's great with people. I'll deal with the rest. Bookkeeping, ordering, whatever you need."

Gemma snugged up to his side. "You sure?" she whispered.

"Absolutely." He squeezed her hand, then backed toward the door. "I'll go get us some coffee. Who's in?"

Marquetta's tight expression relaxed into a smile. "Me, please."

"Me too," Gemma added.

When he returned with watery coffees and pastries from the vending machine, he found Zora snoring softly while Marquetta and Gemma whispered in the corner. Marquetta murmured something to Gemma and gave her a poke. Gemma covered her mouth and giggled. That merry sound was reward enough for whatever extra work he'd do until Zora recovered.

They stayed a few minutes more until the shift nurse announced the end of visiting hours.

Gemma gave Marquetta another hug before looping her arm through Jesse's and moving toward the door.

"Where do you think you're going, young man?" Marquetta called in her best librarian voice.

"I'm taking Gemma home."

"Not without this, you aren't." Marquetta squeezed him in a hug so tight it brought tears to his eyes. Or maybe it was the resemblance to his grandma's hugs that had him all mushy. It had been a helluva day for his heart.

After dropping an exhausted Gemma at Zora and Marquetta's house and promising to bring her Jeep the next morning, Jesse steered for home, his head buzzing like a hive. He hardly recognized himself tonight, first nearly opening heaven's gates with Gemma, then committing to manage a second business for as long as Zora needed. Quick decisions were not his strength. It took him months to ask Shauna out, and even longer—too long, actually—to ask her to move in with him. Now he was hurtling into new connections at warp speed. Scary stuff. Thrilling, too.

He pulled into his parking spot, shut off the truck, and chuckled. "Guess Gemma succeeded in opening my mind."

Chapter Seven

♥

Jesse Del Toro baffled the hell out of Gemma. Two weeks after their interrupted make-out session, he showed no signs of picking things up where they'd left off. True, he stopped by the shop every day and brought her little treats—sweets from Sweet Dreams bakery, kebabs from Ali Baba's, a breakfast frittata from Cassie's Café, not to mention his own homemade tea bread, soup, and flowers from his greenhouse. Each visit, he made pleasant conversation as he helped around the showroom, asking about her past, her family, her schooling, her plans—then he disappeared into Zora's office to deal with the paperwork. Afterward, he gave her a sweet, lingering kiss, then poof! Gone like a hunky Cinderella fleeing the stroke of midnight.

"I don't get it," she told Margot, her go-to friend for over-the-phone amateur therapy. "I've done everything I can think of to show I want him, short of tackling him in the tie-dye aisle. Am I a lousy kisser? Do I have bad breath?"

Margot barked a laugh. "Can't speak to your kissing skills, but your breath is fine, as I recall."

"It's like he's putting me through some kind of trial."

"So tell him."

"Tell him what, exactly?"

Food wrappers crinkled from Margot's end. "That you want him, but you don't understand his mixed messages."

Ah, but such blatant honesty set her up for rejection, just like—*Holy cats!* Until this moment, she hadn't thought of Caleb in... how long? Not since the night of Zora's accident, at least.

Enough childish petulance. Time to woman up and confront the beast.

"Margot, you have a knack for unpeeling the truth. I'll call him tonight. Thanks." She smooched her phone. "Miss you muy mucho much."

"Miss you too, love. See you at the expo."

"Can't wait." She pocketed her phone and sighed. Unlike most of her ex-friends in Eugene whom she'd met through Caleb, Margot remained a steadfast, if long-distance ally. She missed their lingering visits over coffee, their nights of cruising art galleries and bars, their sushi orgies with Olivia and Sierra. The urge to hop into her Jeep and drive south for a quick visit tugged hard on her gut.

No time for that, alas. Not with her responsibilities here. Visiting friends would have to wait until Zora recovered.

The doorway bell tinkled as her four o'clock divination appointment bustled through.

Janice, owner of a Main Street art gallery, was one of Zora's tarot regulars. Gemma's skills with the cards couldn't match her aunt's, so she offered palmistry as an alternative, and a surprising number of customers signed up.

Good thing Nabila Abadi, wife of Mo and co-owner of Ali Baba's Kebabs, volunteered to take a turn at the till today. She greeted Janice, then hollered for Gemma in her foghorn voice.

Gemma pocketed her phone and hurried to the counter. "Thanks again, Nabila. Don't know why we're so busy this afternoon, but I'm grateful for the customers, and for your help."

Nabila tossed her thick salt and pepper hair. "No need to thank me, darling. We miss Zora and Marquetta at our poker group. Besides, Mo can handle the restaurant for an afternoon, and I needed a change of scene. Too much of the same old same old can drive a woman coo-coo. Am I right?" She plucked a pair of beaded earrings from the jewelry case and held them to her cheek, vamping in front of the countertop mirror.

Gemma led Janice behind the wooden screen and poured her a mug of fragrant herbal tea. Not long ago, she'd have agreed with Nabila about the coo-coo bit. How much longer would this new routine amuse her before her feet got itchy again? If not for Zora's illness, she would've stayed for the expo, then—what? For the first time in as long as she could remember, no exciting alternative leapt to mind, and that worried her. Had she lost her mojo, her limitless supply of possibilities? Was she becoming, Goddess forbid, rooted?

Probably just sexual frustration dragging her down.

The bell tinkled again, jerking Gemma's gaze toward the entrance. Sure enough, Jesse was here for his late afternoon visit to check the books. He deposited a tray of green plants on the counter and chatted with Nabila, his rumbling laughter making it damn hard to concentrate on Janice's palms.

Janice sipped her tea. "Thanks for fitting me in, doll. I've got a big decision to make."

Gemma started in on the hand massage that always preceded a reading. For pale-skinned people like Janice, it flushed the palm's lines, making them more visible, and it relaxed the customers too. Much cheaper than therapy.

"You know," she told Janice, "Palmistry is more about understanding yourself than guiding your decisions."

Janice flapped her free hand. "That's fine, hon. Maybe trying something new will give me clarity. I mean, Floyd is a sweetheart, and he's good in bed—great, actually—but art is my passion, and he just doesn't get it. I can't help wondering if I'm wasting my time with him."

"Mmm hmm. That's a toughie." Gemma rubbed circles on Janice's palm while sneaking glances at Jesse. He'd shed his coat, and as he stood on tiptoe to reach a case of earrings from a high shelf, his shirt rode up. The flex of his lower-back muscles sent her pulse into overdrive.

Flushing hot, she yanked her focus to the older woman's hand. "Your heart line is all over the place, frankly. But your head line is strong and straight. Perhaps you're not the settling down type. You might consider—"

Janice gasped. "Oh my God, there he is."

"Who?"

Janice peered around the screen. "Floyd. He's looking through the window. He's never mentioned this shop. What's he doing here? Is it a sign?"

Gemma shrugged. "It could be."

Grinning, Janice dropped a twenty on the table. "Thanks, doll. You've been a big help." She straightened her velvet tunic and quick-stepped toward her boyfriend. By the time Gemma cleaned up the tea mug, she found the older couple holding hands, huddled over the incense display.

Gemma chuckled. Seems Janice had already made up her mind about Floyd. She simply needed a nudge.

Jesse caught her eye, hooked his thumbs into his pockets, and strolled toward her with a smoldering smile on his too-damn-handsome face. Unfair of him to look so delectable here in the shop where she couldn't touch him—at least not the way she wanted to.

He halted with his boot toes inches from hers. "I stopped by Zora and Marquetta's place and left a little something for you on your bed."

She flinched at the mention of bed. Because hunky gorgeousness.

Jesse's brow furrowed. "What's wrong?"

She shook off the image of him stretched out on her lumpy twin mattress. "Nothing. Nice of you to look in on her."

Recalling Courtney's advice, she drew him behind the screen, gulped a deep breath, and faced him. "Listen, did I do something wrong?"

"What do you mean?"

Oh, this is so freakin' hard!

"Well, before Zora fell, you and me, we almost—"

Jesse's smile blazed like the sun. "Yeah, we almost did."

"But for the past week, you've been—"

He raised an eyebrow.

"Distant, I guess."

His smile flattened. "I've been here every day. Yesterday, I brought you dried chamomile. The day before, I brought chocolate mint. Before that..."

"Yes, and thank you. But you only stay a few minutes, then you go home alone."

A corner of his mouth ticked up as he brushed a wisp of hair from her cheek, triggering full-body shivers. "You've missed me?"

Discombobulated by his intoxicating nearness, Gemma spluttered, "Well, I thought...I mean, we shared a moment, and I hoped..."

"You want to see where it goes?" Chuckling, he ran a fingertip over her jaw.

Her nipples pebbled. Breathless, all she could do was nod.

Breaking the spell, Jesse stepped back and shoved his hands into his pockets. "Listen, you've been through a lot lately—Zora's illness, the pacemaker surgery, plus your breakup, and—"

Gemma grabbed his arm. "Zora told you about Caleb?"

He winced and pinched the bridge of his nose. "Mea culpa. I've been asking your aunts about you."

"Why not ask me, Jesse? I'm right here."

He bit his lip, a distractingly sexy gesture. "I've been reading up on Aquarius people. You don't really like talking about your feelings, and—"

"Hold up. Mr. I-Don't-Believe-In-Woo-Woo-Stuff has been studying astrology?"

He shrugged. "You do believe in it, and so does Zora, so I figured it wouldn't hurt to learn more about where you're coming from."

Gemma didn't know whether to laugh or cry. "Holy cats, Jesse. I've been sitting here alone, worrying that you've lost interest, and you're doing research? Can't we just cut to the chase?"

With a low laugh, Jesse glanced over his shoulder, then placed his lips a hair's breadth from her ear. "Get naked, you mean? Is that what you want?"

She hooked her fingers into his hip pockets and tugged him against her. "Yes, please. Ever since that night by the fire, I can't stop thinking about your touch, your voice, your..."

"Gemma." He took her chin between his thumb and forefinger, his expression serious. "You're vulnerable right now. I didn't want to take advantage. If you want to be with me, you need to understand I'm not a casual hookup kind of guy. I have feelings for you, which is pretty damn scary, considering you're all set to bolt from Trappers Cove as soon as Zora is well."

Gemma sighed. "I haven't decided what I'll do when she's well."

That admission was all it took to rekindle his smile. "Look, I'm not proposing. I'm not even asking you to move in. But before I do all the things I want to do to you, I need to know I'm more than a way to pass the time until you leave." His fingers skimmed down her throat, over her collar bones—and just like that, she discovered her new favorite erogenous zone.

"What do you say, Gemma? You ready to take a leap of faith?" He pressed a kiss to her temple and murmured, "Because when you're ready, I'll love you with my hands, my tongue, my cock. I'll fuck you so good you won't ever want to leave me."

Dizzy and trembling, she clutched his shirt to keep from tumbling to the floor.

He nibbled her earlobe, his breath hot against her skin. "You're not there yet, Gemma. And I won't give you what we both want until you let your guard down." His hand slid down to squeeze her hip. "What do you say? Are you ready to be real with me?"

Her hammering heartbeat echoed at the juncture of her thighs. Hard to speak, much less think, with this storm of emotion blowing through her. Aroused, frustrated, and confused, she glided her hands over his firm chest. "Why does this have to be a big thing, Jesse? Can't we just be friends who fool around?"

He speared her with a burning gaze. "I'm not built that way. You've stirred up something powerful in me. I won't be satisfied with just a taste."

The tip of his tongue traced a slow path across his full, bitable lower lip, and her resistance crumbled. "Okay. You win."

"No, my fairy queen." He raised her hand to his lips and kissed her knuckles. "If I get what I want, we both win. See you tonight. My place."

"Should I bring the wine again?"

Fire flickered in his wicked smile. "Just bring your lovely self." He ambled toward the door and called over his shoulder, "And a toothbrush."

Gemma grabbed a display stand to keep from swooning.

Chapter Eight

♥

Jesse checked his recipe for the twentieth time, even though Grandma's lasagna was a dish he could make with his eyes closed. Tomato sauce perfumed with home-grown basil, marjoram, and oregano, sausage made with fennel, fresh-ground white pepper and nutmeg in the bechamel sauce. He'd improvised a pesto from garlic and herbs to spread on crusty peasant bread. Hopefully, this many carbs wouldn't make them too sleepy for—well, time would tell if tonight was the right moment to fulfill the dreams he'd nurtured ever since the night of Zora's accident. Though he craved Gemma with every cell of his body, their first time together was too special to be rushed.

She'd be here any minute. He removed his sauce-splashed apron and made a slow turn to check all the details. Candles set in jars and vases around the kitchen and living room. Fresh flowers bundled with fragrant herbs from his greenhouse: apple mint, rosemary, and lavender-hued roses, a symbol of love at first sight. He'd looked it up. Hopefully, Gemma would get the reference, because telling her flat out how over the moon he felt was terrifying.

He lowered the volume on his smoky blues playlist. As he stepped to the window, a saxophone moaned.

"You and me both, man," he muttered. No picturesque firepit tonight—way too blustery and wet outside. Everything hinged on creating the right atmosphere in his simple farmhouse—sensual, comfortable, the kind of place that makes a woman want to take off her clothes and stay for more. Lots more.

The doorbell finally rang. He sucked in a deep breath, whispered a prayer, and opened it.

A gust of rainy wind lifted Gemma's hair like wings and propelled her into his arms.

"Holy cats." Laughing, she stepped back to remove her sopping raincoat. "Sorry. Got you all wet."

Not as wet as I'm gonna make you by the end of tonight.

Biting his lip, he hung her coat and scarf by the door, then fetched towels to blot her dripping hair. She toed off her rain boots, revealing colorful, hand-knit socks, the kind you wear at home for a cozy night in. The sight twisted his heart.

Down, boy. Dinner first. Don't want her to feel rushed or used. Although judging by her reaction when he kissed her in the shop, she was as hungry for him as he was for her.

Fortunately, Shauna had left behind an old blow dryer. By the time Gemma emerged from the bathroom, her hair fell in thick, dry waves over her shoulders, and damn if she wasn't the most delectable woman he'd ever beheld, dressed for relaxation with just a touch of seduction. Her soft, fuzzy sweater hugged her curves and drew his eye to the shadow of cleavage visible at the neckline. Velvet leggings outlined her shapely thighs and calves.

He pressed a kiss to her forehead. Safe territory. No mauling until after dinner.

"You look beautiful, Gemma." He skimmed his palm down the curve of her side. "You're very fit, aren't you?"

Her cheeks flushed rose pink. "I do a lot of yoga. Helps me chill out."

An image flashed in his mind's eye—Gemma in a down dog position, her ass in the air. His cock pressed hard against his zipper.

He tugged his shirt away from his neck and beckoned her into the kitchen. "Hope you don't mind another simple meal."

She inhaled deeply. "Smells divine."

Grinning, he filled her plate. "Probably not as sophisticated as what you're used to."

She took a bite, closed her eyes, and moaned. At this rate, his poor dick was going to have permanent zipper marks.

"Really good, Jesse." Her smile looked sincere, at least. "And I like all kinds of food. Hey, you should come over to Zora and Marquetta's sometime. I'd love to cook for you."

"Yeah?" His heart leapt, his reaction way out of proportion for an invitation to dine with two old gals. "What'll you make?"

"Hmm." She tapped her sauce-smeared lips. "Maybe Maafe. Ever heard of it?"

He shook his head. *I've gotta be the most boring guy you've ever met.*

"Not surprised." She nabbed another slice of garlic bread. "It's a stew from Senegal. There's peanut butter in the sauce. It's delish."

"I'd love to try it." He topped up both their wine glasses. "So, tell me about your life outside of Trappers Cove."

Her eyes sparkled and danced as she regaled him with descriptions of her mom's suburban house in Olympia, her dad's fishing cabin up in Birch Bay, near Canada, her brother's condo in downtown Austin, jobs she'd worked in Seattle, Tacoma, and Eugene. Her love of travel shone in her happy chatter, but the more excited she got, the lower his heart sank.

Gemma was a vagabond, a true rolling stone. His simple, rooted life could never compete with the allure of the open road.

"Hey." Her soft hand fell on his and squeezed. "I'm sorry. I get carried away with my enthusiasm. Tell me about your favorite places."

He huffed a dry, humorless laugh. "My favorite place is right here. You already know that."

"Of course." Her smile shrank as if he'd chastised her. "What's your favorite spot in Trappers Cove?"

He pushed his empty plate away. "Ivan's Hollow, of course."

She gave him a blank look.

"That little cove you can only access at low tide. Don't you remember?"

"Remember what?"

After three weeks of almost daily contact, she still hadn't mentioned that long-ago summer. That stung, but it wasn't fair to assume it meant as much to her as it did to him. *Tread carefully.*

"I was eighteen, so you must've been sixteen. Your hair was lighter then. You were visiting Zora, I think. You came to the hollow with your cousin Lina. There was a campfire, s'mores, cheap beer. My friend Ryan played guitar. You and Lina started singing along, and I was fuckin' mesmerized."

He reached across the table and took her hand. "I watched the firelight turn your hair to gold, and I couldn't breathe."

Even now, firelight did magical things to Gemma. The flickering candle flame gilded her hair and danced in her blue-green-gray eyes like sunset on the ocean.

He sighed, the beautiful memory squashed by remembered defeat. "Then some out-of-town dude from the campground sat beside you, and by the end of the night, you left with him."

Her hand flew to her lips. "Oh my god, you remember that night? I locked down that memory and never opened the box again." She pantomimed turning a key. "That guy was a monster! He tried to force Lina and me into his car." She brushed a chunk of hair from his forehead. "I remember you now—the sweet guy with the chocolate eyes and the curl that flopped onto his forehead. To think I could've been with you instead of that asinine frat boy." She stroked his cheek. "I'm so sorry, Jesse." Her eyes narrowed. "Wait, when did you recognize me?"

Careful, or you'll sound like a stalker. He gave her a sheepish grin. "I've spotted you in town a few times over the years, but you didn't recognize me, so..." He shrugged, embarrassed to admit how intimidated he'd been. "The memory of that night slapped me across the face when I walked into Zora's shop last month and saw you, your hair all golden under that paper lantern. But I wasn't a hundred percent sure until I asked Zora if you have a Cousin Lina."

He chuckled weakly. "Hope that doesn't make me sound like a creeper. I promise, I haven't been trying to track you down all these years. It's just—extraordinary that you showed up again. Seems like an omen."

Head tilted, she held his gaze in an awkward pause that stretched on and on.

He cleared his throat. "So, what does one wear to an Esoteric Arts Expo? One of those poofy Renn Faire shirts?"

Her laughter snapped the tension as she tossed a hunk of garlic toast at him. He caught it mid-air and gobbled it.

She wiped her hands on her napkin, scooted closer, and laid her hand on his thigh. "Wear that chambray shirt you wore when we first met at Zora's shop. The one that hugs your muscles." Her fingertips skated higher. "That'll drive all the women wild—probably some of the guys too. We'll sell out in an hour."

He placed his hand over hers to still its wandering. "I'm not trying to seduce all the women, just one in particular."

"Mission accomplished." She hooked her leg over his and kissed the side of his neck, firing his blood with the feathery brush of her lips. Much more of this, and he'd explode in his jeans like a teenager.

He extricated himself and scooted his chair back. "Now, now, we haven't had dessert."

Her teasing smile flattened when he returned from the kitchen with an old-fashioned canning jar and slices of sponge cake from Sweet Dreams Bakery.

"Oh, you meant actual dessert." She swiped a hand down her glowing face. "Sorry, Jesse. Who's the creeper now?"

"Don't be sorry. I'm looking forward to tasting you, but I want you to taste this first." He popped the hinged lid and spooned fruit and amber liquid over each slice. "Mirabelle plums in plum wine with rosemary. These are hard to get in this country. My grandfather smuggled some pits back from France after the war. He planted a stand of trees behind the old barn."

He lifted a spoonful to her mouth. Holding his gaze, she sipped the golden treasure, closed her eyes, and released a moan that nearly undid him.

"Here, you've got a dribble." With a fingertip, he wiped the corner of her lips.

She gripped his wrist. Her pink tongue licked the sweetness from his skin, and then—*God save me*—she sucked his finger into the slick warmth of her mouth.

Chapter Nine

♥

Damn it, Jesse, how long are you going to keep me waiting?

If Gemma had to take matters into her own hands, she would. The way his eyes darkened as she laved his finger with her tongue left no doubt that he wanted her. Frustrated with his teasing slowness, she released him and gripped the hem of her sweater. But before she could pull it over her head, he tugged her to her feet.

"I love this song. Dance with me." Drawing her into his arms, he swayed her backward into the living room, where flames crackled in the fireplace. She'd have preferred the bedroom, but at least he was pressed against her, the length of his muscly body heating her front while the fire warmed her back. Stepping onto something soft, she glanced down.

A fluffy fleece rug. *Thank you, Goddess.*

"Just a moment." Jesse stepped to a bar cabinet in the corner.

She gnashed her jaws in horny anguish. Would she have to tackle him and peel his clothes off with her teeth?

He filled two brandy snifters with liquid the color of his eyes. "Homemade apple brandy."

She was about to gulp hers down, but his gentle hand stayed the motion. "Sip it slowly. Like this."

He took a sip, licked his lips, then kissed her deeply, his tongue spiced with cinnamon and the delicious burn of brandy. She chased the sweetness into his mouth, drunk on his heat and strength.

With a rumbling moan, he clutched her hair, tipped her head backward, and drizzled liquor down her throat to pool in the hollow between her collarbones. His velvet tongue lapped it up. The soft wet slide and the rough scrape of his beard electrified her skin.

"Please, Jesse." Her whole body and mind melted into pulsing desire.

"Brandy's even better warmed by the fire." He set their glasses on the hearth, pulled her back into his arms, and resumed their swaying rhythm. With a groan of impatience, she reached for his cock. But as soon as her fingertips brushed the rigid shaft, he seized her hand and lifted it behind his neck. "First, we dance."

Surrendering to his slow seduction was the only way to get what she craved, so she relaxed into his unhurried tempo. He rewarded her by pressing his erection against her in slow, delicious thrusts, one hand splayed on her lower back, the other cradling her head as he seared her mouth with languid kisses.

With agonizing slowness, his fingers slid beneath her sweater, raising trails of goosebumps despite the fire's toasty heat. Round and round his fingertips swirled, teasing her nerves to crackling awareness, skating right to the edge of her bra, then away.

Her head lolled back on a groan.

With a wicked smile, he gripped the hem of her top and whisked it over her head. His gaze heated her skin more than flames ever could. "So beautiful, all golden in the firelight."

At last, he released his hold and let her unbutton his shirt. It fell open to reveal his sculpted torso, his chest and stomach dusted with dark hair that tickled deliciously against her breasts, his back satin smooth and hot beneath her hands.

Holding her gaze, he lifted her thigh, fingers digging into her flesh as he bent her backward in a dramatic dip. His eyes burned into hers—then his lips twitched, his ribs shook, and he snorted a laugh.

"You goof." Giggling, she punched his shoulder.

"Damn it, woman, I'm trying to be romantic." Still chuckling, he lowered her onto the fleece and covered her body with his, pressing their foreheads together. "I meant what I said, Gemma. This is more than play to me. This means something. We don't have to define it now, but we're more than just friends." He drew so close, only a whisper of charged air separated his lips from hers. "Do you feel the same, or should I stop?"

She remembered the words he growled into her ear that afternoon. "I'll fuck you so good you won't ever want to leave me."

Flutters shook her belly. *This is crazy. I've known him less than a month.* A small, craven part of her wanted to flee, but deep in her gut, she knew that would be a mistake. She and Jesse were meant to meet. He had something to teach her, and she was going to enjoy every second of the learning process. Starting now.

"I'm ready for you, Jesse." She wrapped her legs around his hips and pulled him to her. "Unleash your inner bull."

Another laugh from him, followed by a moan as he ground his hardness against her sex. One thrust, two, then he slid down, removing the object of her desire from the place she needed it most.

"Nooo. Come back."

"So impatient." He nuzzled the crook of her neck, alternating soft kisses, sharp nips, and velvety licks, a cascade of contrasting sensations. "We have all night. Let me enjoy discovering you."

Again, she reached for him, but he pinned her wrists above her head with one hand and feathered kisses over her breasts through her bra, just enough to tease, before nibbling down her stomach, finally releasing her to tug her leggings over her hips.

She reached down to help him, but he pushed her hands away. So that was his game—whenever she tried to hurry him, he deliberately slowed. Normally, she hated being confined or controlled, but there was no denying her body's response to this sensual battle of wills.

"Let go, Gemma," he murmured, his voice somewhere between a purr and a growl. "Let yourself feel. We have all the time in the world."

But she couldn't promise him that, couldn't share his confidence in their future, and letting him think otherwise was cruel. Buffeted by conflicting emotions, she clenched her teeth and tried to recapture the moment.

"You're getting lost in your head again. Let me loosen you up." He rolled her onto her stomach and peeled her leggings all the way off.

She watched his jeans fall to the floor, revealing powerful thighs dusted with dark hair, and an impressive erection straining against tight black boxer briefs.

Moaning, she reached for him, but he spread her body on the fleece rug like a baker kneading dough. "Let me have this pleasure, Gemma. Let me memorize every beautiful inch of you. Afterward, you can have your impatient way with me, I promise. But I need this." He pressed kisses down her back as his strong hands coaxed all the stiffness from her muscles until she lay pliant, panting, completely at his mercy. Soft fluff beneath her, powerful fingers molding her flesh, opening her, his hot breath on her nape, the gentle rasp of his thigh nudging her legs further apart. He slid his fingers inside her panties to massage her ass cheeks, then trailed a finger over her hyper-sensitive sex. Each touch jolted her like an electric shock.

"I want you so bad, Jesse," she groaned into the fleece.

"Not as bad as I want you, lovely one." He gifted her a few delicious thrusts against her ass. She lifted to meet him, and his hand slipped beneath her to massage her folds, expertly zeroing in on her clit.

She reached back and clutched his side, fingernails digging into firm muscle. "I need you inside me."

"Soon, my fairy queen." The warmth of his body disappeared. A drawer opened and closed. Breathless, she waited for the crinkle of a condom wrapper, but instead she heard a click, followed by the swish of Jesse's hands rubbing together. Straddling her, he massaged her arms and shoulders with sweet-smelling oil that transformed his touch into a gliding wonder.

With a deft flick of his fingers, he unhooked her bra and smoothed oil over her back and teased the outer curve of her breasts. He leaned into her with perfect pressure and glided his palms down her sides, hooking the waistband of her panties along the way. He slid them off, gently lifting one leg, then the other, and tossed away the scrap of satin and lace. He massaged the arches of her feet and slid his oiled fingers between her toes. She'd never considered her feet an erogenous zone, but giddy sensations danced up her legs and pulsed in her core.

He rose again, kneading the sensitive skin of her inner thighs before finally, thank the Goddess, sliding his fingers between her sopping folds. She lifted her hips to give him better access, and he gripped them, shifting to press his face where his fingers had been. His beard scraped her flesh deliciously as his tongue flicked and stroked. Within seconds, climax roared through her, as forceful as a mighty ocean wave. She keened and writhed against him, but he kept up his delicious, merciless assault until she collapsed, helpless and spent.

At last, she heard the crinkle of foil and a feral snarl as Jesse rose on his knees, pulled her hips to his and, in one brutal thrust, impaled her on his sheathed cock. Shockwaves of pleasure ricocheted through her body. Her oiled back slid against his furry chest and belly. His slippery hands cupped and squeezed her breasts, rolling her nipples as he ground in deep.

"Look, Gemma," he growled into her ear. "See how beautiful you are."

She hadn't noticed the mirrored cabinet until this moment. Jesse's reflected gaze burned into hers. And she felt beautiful, her hair wild, plastered to her face and tangled in his beard, her skin flushed, her mouth gaping wide, her back arched to meet his thrusts. He angled her body so they could watch his thick shaft churning in and out of her flesh. The sight stoked her arousal and sped her movements.

"No, angel. Don't force me to come yet." Gripping her more firmly, he slowed his movements and stroked her clit in feather-light touches. "From the moment I saw you in Zora's shop, I've craved this."

Tremors wracked her body, but he kept his touch so light she trembled on the edge, her climax shimmering just out of reach.

Time for a dose of his own medicine.

"I wanted you too, Jesse," she growled over her shoulder, "from the minute you pierced me with those intense dark eyes." Reaching back, she raked her fingers into his hair. "These silky curls, your muscly shoulders, that sexy way you snort. I knew, this man is a bull. He's going to absolutely slay me with his hot, thick cock. I can't wait to taste him, to feel him moving inside me..."

His control slipped at last. With a grunt, he pushed her onto hands and knees and covered her back with his body. His thrusts grew faster, his rhythm ragged, his panting breath hot on her back as he fucked her with rough passion. Heat licked down her spine. His fingers dug into her shoulder as he bellowed her name, and she answered him with a scream as pleasure slammed through her.

When the shock of bliss subsided, she found herself face-down on the fleece rug with Jesse curled around her, his heavy thigh thrown over her sweat-slicked body. Every inch of her hummed and throbbed in time with his heartbeat.

Still breathing hard, he murmured her name over and over and skated his fingertips over her skin in delicious spirals. He slid out of her, drawing a mewl of disappointment.

"Sorry. Gotta clean up." He kissed her nape. Footsteps padded away.

She really ought to get up, but the fire's heat was so lovely on her back, the fleece so soft beneath her side, she couldn't summon the will to move.

Jesse returned with a fluffy towel. Gently, he blotted between her legs and wiped the oil from her skin with long strokes. Afterward, he sat beside her, still gloriously nude, and reached for their glasses. "See? It's perfectly warm now."

"As hot as that was, I'm surprised the brandy didn't combust." Rising on one elbow, she sipped the sweet, spicy liquor, then stretched again, her muscles buttery soft and completely relaxed. He spooned against her side, his fingertips skating over her skin. Normally, she was too sensitized after sex to enjoy further caresses. But her usual urge to cover herself and flee never arrived. Wonder of wonders, Jesse Del Toro had taught her to appreciate post-sex cuddles.

He shifted onto his back, pulling her over him like a blanket. Heady stuff, the sensation of his big, hot body beneath her, his steady heartbeat against her cheek. While he hummed into her hair, she glanced down at his cock, still half-erect against his thigh. So many things she wanted to do with this gentle bull of a man—suck him till he begged for release, ride him slow, then fast and hard, wake up cradled in his arms, linger over morning coffee in his sunny, rustic kitchen, work side by side in that oxygen-rich greenhouse, his quiet presence soothing as she sank her fingers into the soil…

The vision was so clear she jerked in his tender hold. Where the hell did that thought come from?

"What is it, love? Are you uncomfortable? Cold?"

Just spooked by visions of a future that'll never happen.

With a sigh soaked in regret, she nestled against his chest. "We didn't even make it to your bedroom."

He pressed a kiss to her temple. "Got another fireplace in there." He nibbled the shell of her ear. "And a big, four-poster bed. Next time, I'll tie you to the posts and lick you until you forget every word but my name."

She shivered in his arms, half from anticipated pleasure, and half from fear of being tied down—not literally, because being restrained and sweetly tortured by Jesse sounded absolutely thrilling. But if one climax with him—okay, two, almost three if she counted their encounter by his fire pit—anyhow, if this first taste of Jesse's love reduced her to a boneless, brainless blob, what would happen when her itchy feet pulled her out of his orbit? Could this surprise connection survive a separation? Or would she end up hurting him like she'd hurt Caleb?

Why did he have to be so sweet and attentive? So passionate and sure? Fate was cruel to pick this moment, when her world tumbled and slid beneath her feet, to introduce this dangerous man who tempted her to make promises her vagabond heart could never keep? Jesse held the power to split her soul wide open. Would the Gemma she knew survive?

Chapter Ten

♥

Jesse's patience paid off. Over the next few weeks, he and Gemma fell into a comfortable rhythm, meeting up daily at the shop to deal with business matters before ducking behind the wooden screen for fevered kisses. Some nights, he joined her at Zora and Marquetta's for dinner and card games. Other times, he cooked for her before jumping her beautiful bones.

Knowing her distaste for routine, he took care to ravish her in each room of his house—bent over the kitchen table, sprawled on the sofa, slippery under the shower, or tied spread-eagled to his four-poster bed—without a doubt, the hottest sexual experience of his life. As always, she fought to speed his tempo and race toward climax, but she never once used her safe word. Tying her up let him prolong their pleasure and relish every inch of her luscious body with hands, tongue and teeth before finally unleashing himself in a flurry of frantic thrusts that drove them both over the edge. Even now, the memory of her nails raking his back as her inner walls clutched his cock brought an instant hard-on.

Afterward, she'd teased him. "Do you always stock your room with silk scarves for tying up women?"

"Actually, I bought these for you. Don't you dare tell Annabelle what we used them for. I'll never be able to face her again." Come to think of it, the antiques vendor had looked at him funny as she rang up a half dozen scarves. She probably knew.

He kissed his way down to Gemma's breasts. "Want to try the greenhouse next time? I'll bring an air mattress."

Laughing, she ruffled his hair. "As big and rough as you are, we'd pop it for sure."

"I'll bring a patch kit."

The astrology books he'd read warned him that Aquarius women wanted each date to be a new adventure—hard to do with his responsibilities on the farm, plus the extra work to keep Zora's shop running. But Gemma was worth every meticulous detail. This time around, he'd do whatever it took to hold her interest. Unlike his time with Shauna, he'd never assume Gemma was comfortable and content just because he was.

And he was comfortable. Talking with her, working side by side, sharing companionable meals, even if his cooking was far more boring than her exotic curries and stir-fries—it all came so easily. Secretly, he worried about that old saying—when something seems too good to be true, it probably is. But for now, Gemma hadn't mentioned plans to leave Trappers Cove. If he could keep her intrigued until after the Esoteric Arts Expo in two weeks, he had a fighting chance.

He rechecked the weather report before packing the last treats for tonight's date. The angels must be looking out for him because low tide would arrive at the perfect time, allowing them to watch the sunset from Ivan's Hollow, the hidden cove where he'd first spotted Gemma. Hopefully, the chilly February temps would keep other lovers away, and they'd have the pristine little beach to themselves. In case they got lucky, he'd packed his truck with a thermos of hot tea, a picnic of quesadillas from Ryan's bar and cookies from Garrett's bakery, plus firewood, blankets, lube, wipes, and sturdy camp chairs—because everyone who grew up in a coastal town knew the importance of elevating sensitive body parts above the sand.

At four-thirty, he picked Gemma up and thanked Nabila and Janice, who'd agreed to close the shop. Seems he wasn't the only one eager to convince Gemma to stay in Trappers Cove.

He found her with her delectable ass in the air, bent over a low shelf. After a long moment of ogling and thanking his lucky stars, he cleared his throat. "Evening, Gemma. You ready?"

Grinning, she hopped to her feet. "Let's go." She pecked the older women's cheeks and admonished them, "Now, don't you let Zora sneak in here while I'm gone. Doc told her two more weeks of relaxing at home."

Nabila elbowed her friend and saluted. "Aye aye, mon capitaine."

"Bossy, isn't she?" Janice added with a wink. "Sure you can handle her?"

Biting her lip, Gemma caught his eye and giggled. Though a take-charge woman in most aspects of her life, she seemed to be enjoying his dominant ways in the bedroom—or whichever room they found themselves in when their clothes came flying off.

He boosted Gemma into his pickup, then drove onto the beach, deserted except for a few anglers. Evening sun gilded the gentle surf. He steered toward the packed sand at the shoreline and around the natural rock wall that separated Ivan's Hollow from the main beach. Huzzah and hallelujah, the little cove was empty.

"Wow," Gemma exclaimed as she hopped down. "All this gorgeousness for us?"

"For the next three hours or so. We'll have to head back if we don't want to spend the night." As he hefted their gear from the truck's bed, he cursed himself for not attaching the camper shell he hadn't used since taking over the farm.

Gemma made a slow *Sound of Music* turn, arms wide. "I forgot how beautiful this place is. Haven't been out here since that summer in high school."

"Well, that's a damn shame." He spread a waterproof tarp on the sand before unfolding their camp chairs and blankets.

She eyed the set-up warily. "Looks like you're expecting a storm."

"Just want you to be comfortable." He unpacked a folding shovel and inclined his head toward the truck. "Shall we set up for dinner? There's a camp table in the back."

Soon, he had a fire crackling and a satisfied smile on his face as Gemma oohed and aahed over their picnic. Call him a caveman, but he loved providing for her.

"What's in the foil packets? They smell so good."

"Quesadillas from the Salty Dog Saloon—smoked gouda with wild mushrooms, and blackened shrimp with bacon and avocado. There's salad in the Tupperware."

She nuzzled his neck. "You are totally spoiling me, you know."

Her delicate touch sparked a squadron of fireflies in his belly. "I aim to please."

He helped her set the table, then popped the cork on a chilled Columbia Valley Pinot Gris. He wasn't much of a wine guy himself, but she'd mentioned loving this stuff, and he was determined to impress her.

They settled into their chairs, bundled up in blankets, and feasted on delicious food and glorious color as the sun sank toward the horizon, which flushed a delicate pink before flaring into orange and magenta, its colors mirrored where the sea slicked the sand.

The blazing sky heightened the roses in Gemma's cheeks and illuminated her changeable eyes, sea green tonight in the magical glow of sunset and firelight. She pushed her plate aside and reached for his hand. "Jesse, this is spectacular. Thank you."

Time for a gamble. He twisted to face her. "Is it beautiful enough to hold your interest?"

She held his gaze for a long, silent moment. Seagulls cried and tap-danced toward their campsite, hoping for morsels. The surf whooshed in and out, Mother Earth's soft breath. Jesse chewed his lip and prayed.

Finally, Gemma ducked her head and chuckled. "You and me. What an unlikely pair, eh?"

He wove his fingers through hers. "I think we make an excellent pair."

Her thumb rubbed circles on his palm, a move that would normally soothe him. Not enough to loosen his wire-taut nerves now when everything depended on overcoming her urge to wander.

Her gaze shifted out to sea. "Tell me about your future, Jesse."

"Well, I'm hoping you'll be in it."

She dropped her hand and wrapped her arms around her bent knees, still focused on the sunset as if she couldn't bear to miss a moment of its beauty. That was his Gemma, soaking up every experience like a sponge, always hungry for new sensations, new experiences. Who was he kidding? No beach or sunset or meal or orgasm would ever be enough to hold her here.

In that case, he might as well be truthful. Intuitive as she was, she'd see through lies designed to persuade her. "Okay," he began, "I'd like to have a family of my own. I'm already thirty-six, so I'd better not wait too much longer." He huffed a humorless chuckle. "Guess guys have a biological clock too. But first, I need a partner, one who supports me and challenges me. One who won't let me get too stodgy."

Gemma faced him at last with a cute scowl. "Who says you're stodgy?"

"My last girlfriend."

Her frown relaxed, and she rested her cheek on her knees. "I was wondering if you'd ever tell me about her. A teacher, wasn't she?"

Of course Gemma would've heard all about it in a town this small. "Yeah. She was like you in some ways. Easily bored. I was good enough to pass the time while she was stuck in Trappers Cove—though I never realized she felt stuck here. She seemed happy with the town, her job, me. Then one day, out of the blue, she got an offer from a private school in Seattle. I didn't even know she'd applied." He sighed into the twilight sky. "And that was that. Guess she had—what did you call it? Itchy feet." The longer he spoke, the more his stomach hollowed out. It was only a matter of time until Gemma grew bored and moved on too.

Her hand closed over his, warm and soft. "Well, shame on her for treating you that way. Karma's going to bite her ass one day."

Desperation squirmed under his skin. Turning his body to face her, he enfolded her hand in both of his. "Zora warned me about you, Gemma, but I could no more resist you than I could stop breathing. You're gonna mash my heart to a pulp, aren't you?"

She recoiled. "No. Of course not. I care about you, Jesse, and—wait, Zora warned you?"

"She said our star signs are incompatible."

Gemma's eyes narrowed and her chin firmed. "That's bullshit. We're not helpless puppets, Jesse. We control our own destinies."

"What about your itchy feet?"

She screwed her eyes shut and growled, a distractingly sexy sound. "I wish I'd never used that stupid phrase. All it means is I enjoy variety."

"In your lovers?"

She threw up her hands. "No! I've only ever been with one guy at a time. My ex-boyfriend lasted three years, and he was the one who ended it, not me." She thumped her chest. "And yes, I do like to travel. I have friends up and down the West Coast, and I enjoy spending time with them. Friendship is very important to me."

He flinched at that loaded word. He'd told her he wanted so much more than friendship from her. Had she listened?

Her intense gaze pierced him. "Once I make a friend, that's it. Loyal for life. Not like your flakey girlfriend."

"Or your flakey boyfriend? Because you deserve better. You deserve someone who'll stick by you." He reached for her hand again. She let him take it but didn't squeeze back.

"Why are you with me, Gemma?"

Avoiding his gaze, she picked at crumbs on her blanket. "Besides the earthquake sex, you mean?"

Well, at least he had that point in the plus column. "Yeah, it's pretty spectacular. Best I've ever had, to be honest. But you haven't answered my question."

She shrugged. "You're—intriguing. At first glance, you seem like a simple man, hardworking, loyal, a homebody..."

"In other words, boring."

Her gaze snapped to his. "Damn it, Jesse. Don't put words in my mouth, okay?"

"Sorry. Guess I'm bracing myself for when the axe falls."

Her voice sharpened. "There's no axe. I'm just—" she snarled her frustration. "This is so hard. I've never been good at describing my feelings. I mean, that's why we call them feelings, not explanations. You've gotta feel them. Words aren't big enough."

He squeezed her hand. "Try. Please."

Like a boxer about to step into the ring, she closed her eyes, rotated her shoulders, and huffed. "Okay, here goes."

She shoved the table back, turned so their knees touched, and took both his hands. "You've got me hooked good, Jesse, and I'm not sure why. It's not just the sex, and not just your cooking—which is excellent, by the way. But, except for how breathtakingly gorgeous you are, you're not the kind of guy I ever pictured myself with. And yet, being with you makes me happy, if sometimes frustrated. It's going to take me a while to sort it out, okay?"

Not the answer he was hoping for, but at least a step in the right direction. Clearly, emotional honesty was hard for Gemma. He should cut her some slack.

"Okay." He chuckled. "Take your time. I'll be over here, you know, being gorgeous."

"You beautiful jerk." Laughing, thank God, she socked his shoulder.

"Oho, my beauty likes it rough." Grasping her waist, he pulled her onto his seat, which sank deeper into the sand but didn't collapse under their combined weight.

With a graceful movement, she swung her leg over his body, straddling him. "Interesting suggestion. Maybe I should tie you up, give you a taste of your own kinky medicine." Eyes glittering in the firelight, she rocked her hips against his.

Jesse had never experienced such overpowering beauty. Stars twinkled overhead as the indigo sky gave way to black. Gemma's eyes shone brighter than stars as she arranged blankets to cover them both, then unfastened his shirt and ran her hands over his skin, each silky caress hotter than the next. His cock hardened painfully, and he canted his hips into her softness.

Humming low in her throat, she slid lower and tugged the blankets over her head.

"Babe, I want to see you."

"Don't look," she said, her voice husky and teasing. "Just feel." Kneeling in the sand, she unfastened his belt, opened his jeans, and pulled out his cock. "Hello, beauty," she murmured before drawing it into her mouth.

The firm strokes of her velvet tongue and the scrape of her nails over his balls made his breath shudder and his nerves sing. No one was around to hear, so he gave in to primal instinct, groaning and crying out with each flash of pleasure. Her merciless caresses built layers of sensation, higher and higher until—

The blanket whisked away, revealing Gemma naked from the waist down, her jeans dangling from one ankle, a condom packet between her fingers. She'd picked his pocket, clever girl. Her eyes held a feral gleam as she sheathed him, then straddled him again. Holding his cock firmly by the root, she slid the aching head back and forth between her slick folds. "I need you to make me come. Can you do that, Jesse?"

Gibberish tumbled from his lips as she sheathed him in liquid heat. The sweet, silken grip of her inner flesh filled his mind with stars.

"Give me your hand," she commanded, and placed his thumb over her clit. "Like this." She guided him over the swollen nub. Her breath grew ragged as she rocked her hips back and forth in time with the waves, a gentle sway that held him on the edge of ecstasy.

"Soooo nice," she moaned, increasing her tempo.

He couldn't help rocking up into her as she rode him in the moonlight, firelight painting her bare thighs with tiger stripes. Her hands tunneled under his shirt, raking and clutching his sides. Head thrown back, she keened her pleasure into the night sky. He pressed harder with his thumb, grinding her clit in tight circles and straining to hold back the climax coiled at the base of his spine.

"Jesse. Yes. Now," she panted, then curled forward as her pussy gripped him like a satin-gloved fist. He screamed her name, and his spirit soared into the night sky, dancing with hers while their bodies shuddered below.

Slowly, his mind and body reunited, and he opened his eyes to find Gemma draped across him, her jacket and sweater twisted, her eyes closed in bliss.

Okay, that was just sex, right? Really good sex, but not an actual out-of-body experience on the astral plane.

But no matter how his rational mind scrabbled for an explanation, deep down where the truth lived, Jesse knew this amazing connection was meant to be.

Chapter Eleven

♥

The next week flew by. Zora returned to the shop for half days, her body still fatigued from surgery but her mind buzzing with ideas for the expo, now just a week away. Gemma spent evenings huddled with her aunt over plans for their booth. Transporting all their goods and display materials down to Portland was a huge logistical challenge the likes of which she had yet to experience, since most of her previous work had more to do with herding people.

Jesse came over most evenings. His eye for detail and insistence on back-up plans proved invaluable. But by bedtime, Gemma was wiped out, so their lovemaking dwindled to brief tumbles in his bed. A few nights, when she couldn't even keep her eyes open, Jesse tucked her into Zora's lumpy guest bed, gave her a sweet goodnight kiss, and left her to sleep alone. She missed him on those nights, and the next morning when she woke without his big, toasty body spooned around hers. But soon this expo adventure would be over, and they'd rediscover their rhythm, a process she was looking forward to with great anticipation.

"See you tomorrow night?" He murmured as he tucked her in on Saturday. "I'll make us something special."

"Sounds wonderful." She wound her arms around his neck, kissed him, and nestled into her pillow. It had been a long day at the shop with an unusual number of customers, a broken toilet, a drunk, belligerent palmistry client, and unending phone calls to suppliers who made excuses about late shipments. She was wiped out.

With a chuckle, he whispered, "Sweet dreams, fairy girl," and walked to the door.

"Jesse?" she croaked.

"Yeah, babe?"

"You're a wonderful boyfriend."

He paused in the doorway, holding the frame. As she slid into slumber, she had the funniest thought—Jesse as a sculpted marble figure of Atlas, holding up the roof, keeping her safe and sheltered. Sweet, generous, dependable Jesse. She was lucky to have him.

The next morning, she woke to the scent of pancakes. Confused, she rubbed her eyes and stretched. Jesse made the most wonderful pancakes, but she was in her own bed, not his bigger, comfier one. She slid into her slippers and robe and padded into the kitchen.

A loud, goose-like honking made her jump.

"Happy birthday, darling girl!" Wearing shiny paper hats and tooting party horns, Zora and Marquetta squeezed her in a hug sandwich.

She yawned. "Oh yeah, it's the thirteenth, isn't it?"

Marquetta beamed. "We made your favorite—chocolate chip pancakes with whipped cream."

Honestly, she'd be happier with yogurt and granola, but it was sweet of her aunties to fix her childhood favorite. Since growing up, she didn't pay much attention to birthdays, so a candle stuck into a stack of Marquetta's pancakes was all the fuss she needed. At her age, she certainly wasn't counting on a bouncy castle, a pile of gifts, or a pony, for goodness' sake. Just another day like any other.

"Say, you didn't tell Jesse it's my birthday, did you?"

"Of course not." Zora patted her shoulder. "Although if you ask me, this birthday avoidance quirk of yours is weird. The young man adores you. Let him spoil you a little."

She laughed and wiped whipped cream from her chin. "He spoils me plenty." Not that she'd go into the details of how deliciously he spoiled her—not at her aunties' breakfast table, anyway. "I'll tell him when I see him tonight."

Marquetta shook her head. "Knowing Jesse, he'd want to bake you a cake."

"He always makes a dessert when I come over. We'll just stick a candle in it."

"What about presents?"

"His presence is all the present I need." She batted her eyelashes and flashed a teasing grin. It had taken years to convince her family to stop buying her birthday and holiday gifts. While she appreciated the sentiment, with her itinerant lifestyle, where would she keep all the trinkets?

Better this way. Jesse seemed to be at peace with their differences. He'd understand. And if he insisted on giving her a gift, she'd ask for another of his bone-melting massages. The man truly had magic hands.

Still, as Gemma walked to the shop, an odd, fizzy feeling washed over her, prickling her skin into goosebumps. She froze and glanced around, but no clues presented themselves. The winter sun shone extra bright and sharp, and the ocean's salty scent floated on a brisk wind that whipped her hair into her face. She scraped the errant strands back with both hands, closed her eyes, and focused inward.

Something important was coming her way today. This sensation of premonition always heralded a turning point—but for good or ill?

No answer came, so she continued down Main Street. She'd know soon enough.

The shop was busy for a February Sunday, the fair weather having drawn tourists from inland. No sign of Jesse, who told her he'd be running deliveries to restaurants and markets all day. Had he somehow found out about her birthday? That would explain her hunch. A steady stream of palmistry customers kept her from pondering further.

"Gemma, darling." Zora poked her head around the wooden screen. "Your next customers are here."

She knuckled her eyes. "Customers? I can't do a group reading."

"Surprise!" In a flurry of waving hands and flying hair, Margot, Sierra, and Olivia burst around the screen and lifted her in a group hug.

"You guys!" She couldn't believe her teary eyes. She hadn't seen her girl posse from Eugene since she left Oregon a month ago. "What are you doing here?"

"Celebrating your birthday, of course." Margot blew into a party noisemaker that unfurled its paper tube and bopped her on the nose.

"Bullseye," Sierra squealed. "Here, you wear this." She pulled a "Birthday Princess" tiara from her oversized bag and plopped it onto Gemma's head.

"We got a suite in Portland, baby." Olivia smooched her on both cheeks. "We're gonna paint the town."

Gemma straightened her crown and gave a mighty sniffle. "Goddess, I've missed you guys so much!"

After a month of communicating only on tiny screens, seeing her friends in the flesh filled her heart with giddy warmth. So that's what set off her inner radar. Somehow, she must've sensed their approach.

"I can't believe you drove all this way just to surprise me," she squealed and threw her arms around them again.

And then a chill slithered down her spine. "Oh, but I have a date tonight."

"Cancel it," Margot said with a flip of her hand. "Sisters before misters."

"Now, now, be fair." Olivia, ever the level-headed one, clucked her tongue. "If Gemma has a new fella, she can't just blow him off."

"Right." Sierra nodded. "He can come with us. We've got a table at this new vegan restaurant, and my cousin's getting us into the best club, I swear. Your boyfriend likes to dance, right?"

Gemma sputtered. "Actually, I don't know." Sure, they'd danced in his living room, but that only lasted a few minutes before they got horizontal. Somehow, she couldn't imagine Jesse on a crowded dance floor.

When she lived in Eugene, where she'd met this trio at an art festival, they'd get together at least a couple times a month for a girls' night out. Sometimes, Margot's boyfriend Elmer would come along, and they'd all dance around him in a giggling, bopping scrum of energy and alcohol.

Jesse was a good sport, but she didn't see him enjoying their kind of fun.

"What's that sour look?" Margot scowled. "You're not going to cancel on us, are you?"

She glanced at the clock above the door. Jesse expected her in an hour. He'd understand, wouldn't he? After all, it was her birthday. Why shouldn't she have some fun, a little taste of the life she'd left behind?

She chewed a knuckle. "I just wish you guys had given me a heads up."

"And spoil the surprise?" Olivia pulled a wrapped package from her backpack. "We even brought you something to wear."

"Guys, come on." This was spinning out of control.

"Shut up with your 'I hate presents' bullshit." Impossible to be mad at Margot when she delivered her bossy zingers with a sweet smile. "Besides, we got it at a thrift shop, so it's good for the environment, right?"

"Yeah." Sierra nodded, her arms folded over her low-cut sweater. "It's virtuous repurposing of discarded goods."

"Open it, already." Olivia tapped her booted foot.

Pointless to argue, so she ripped the wrapping paper and pulled out a diaphanous, sparkly tunic in glorious peacock colors of sapphire, emerald, and amethyst.

Her jaw dropped. "This. Is. Gorgeous." She couldn't wait to show Jesse.

Oh. Shit. Jesse.

"Gimme a minute." She tried Jesse's number, but it went to voicemail, so she left him a text.

Friends surprised me for my birthday. Can I get a raincheck for tonight? We'll stop by on our way to Portland.

She almost added **Love you** but froze, her thumbs over the screen. A strange tingle danced across her skin. *Do I love Jesse?* Was that why her intuition lit up this morning?

She shook her head. No, her friends' surprise was the obvious answer. Sorting out her feelings for Jesse could wait twenty-four hours. Maybe some time with her girlfriends would give her perspective. She hit Send and tucked her phone into her pocket, trying to ignore the sharp pinch of guilt.

Olivia, an artist who painted on huge canvases, had brought her Chevy van, and the girls had decked it out in Happy Birthday balloons and streamers. She hopped into the Magic Bus, as they'd christened it, and they headed for Zora's place where Gemma changed into velvet leggings, tall boots, and her new glittery top.

After greeting Gemma's friends, Aunt Zora pulled her aside. "Honey, are you sure you want to do this? Breaking a date with someone who cares about you invites bad karma. Knowing Jesse, he's probably gone to a lot of trouble."

Her aunt's warning layered on another scoop of guilt. "As far as he knows, it's just another Sunday night." Gemma's eyes narrowed. "Unless someone told him about my birthday."

Zora raised her hands, palms out. "Of course we didn't. We respect your wishes. But still, Jesse's going to be hurt."

She closed her eyes and blew out a shaky breath. Aunt Z was right, but what could she do? Her stomach twisted at the thought of disappointing Jesse, but if they had any hope of a future together, he had to understand how important friendship was to Gemma—especially these three who'd comforted her after Caleb said goodbye. Her friends were the family of her heart.

All sparkled up for a night on the town, she climbed into Olivia's van and directed them to Jesse's farm. Still no reply to her text. He must have left his phone in the greenhouse or his pickup.

"Mega cute," Margot said as they rolled up the gravel drive. "Elmer would love this place. Lots of nature, lots of room."

"And look at that sweet little house!" Sierra pointed. "It's like a Christmas card."

In fact, he'd strung fairy lights on the porch. What was that about?

"Are you serious about this guy?" Olivia asked.

"I mean, he's got potential." *Understatement of the year.*

"Is that him?"

Gemma followed Margot's pointing finger to the herb greenhouse, where Jesse stood in the doorway, a wine bottle in his hand.

"Uh oh. Looks like boyfriend had plans for you tonight," Margot muttered. "Guys, we shoulda called."

"It's okay." *No, it's not. How am I going to explain?* Pulse fluttering in near panic, Gemma opened the passenger door and stepped down. "Let me go talk to him." She wrapped the cloak she'd borrowed from Zora around her shoulders and trotted toward him.

"Hello, new boyfriend," Sierra called, hanging half out of the van's window and waving her long arms.

"Shut it, Sisi," Olivia hissed.

Jesse stared at the spectacle, his jaw tight. When his gaze turned on her, hurt and confusion shone in his eyes. "What's going on?"

"I texted you. Didn't you see my message?"

He shook his head. "Reception's spotty out here. And I've been busy." He lifted the wine bottle.

"Shit and double shit. Zora told you, didn't she?"

"Told me what?"

"About my birthday. I asked her not to."

Salsa music blared from the van. The girls were starting the party without her.

"Let's go inside." She stepped around him and into the greenhouse, then froze.

Jesse had transformed the space from farm to fairyland. Flowers bloomed among the herbs and spilled from a crystal vase on a table set for two. Soft music played. Twinkle lights blinked overhead, and paper hearts fluttered in the gentle breeze from the ventilator fans. The whole scene was so romantic...

Holy cats, is he going to propose? Her knees locked. Her vision swam.

Jesse gripped her shoulders. His brows contracted. "Help me understand. Today is your birthday?"

"Yeah." Her chuckle sounded phony even to her own ears. "The big three-four."

"And you didn't tell me?"

"I, uh, don't like to make a fuss. It's just another day, right?"

"Bullshit." His harsh tone jerked her backwards.

"Your birthday is important to me, Gemma. After all we've shared, you should have told me." His wounded stare bored into her, turning her knees to water. Then he turned away.

That's when she spotted the gauzy cloth hung from the rear of the greenhouse, draped like a canopy over—*oh goddess*—an air mattress, piled high with pillows and a fake fur throw. He'd arranged a whole romantic scene, just for her.

She clutched his arm. "Jesse, if you didn't know about my birthday, what is this?"

She didn't like the deep crease between his brows, not one tiny bit.

He closed his eyes and massaged his temples with one hand. "It's for Valentine's Day."

"Oh." Her stomach bottomed out. Of course she knew about that mushy holiday. She'd decorated the shop in pink, red, and purple. She'd arranged a display of love potions and charms, books about attracting love and finding your perfect soulmate, pink crystals and red glass roses and all manner of lovey-dovey merchandise. But she hadn't figured Jesse for the type to make a big romantic gesture.

She swallowed a huge, spiky ball of regret that threatened to choke her. "Valentine's Day isn't until tomorrow, right?"

"I wanted to surprise you." His voice rasped, dry as the Sahara. "I'm trying to give you what you want, Gemma. New experiences.

A change of scene. And you like the greenhouse so much, I thought you'd appreciate this."

Outside, one of the girls leaned on the horn.

His sigh twisted her heart. "Looks like you're not staying."

She clutched his arms. She had to make him understand. "Jesse, I'm so sorry. I hate making a fuss about my birthday, but my friends drove up from Eugene to surprise me. They've arranged a whole night out in Portland. Back in Oregon, whenever one of us was down, we'd go out dancing to cheer her up. They helped me through my breakup with Caleb, and—"

From his blank expression, she might as well be talking to a wall.

She grasped his hand. It lay lifeless in hers. "If I'd known, I would've told them to come another time. They meant well."

His expression hardened. "And you never thought I'd want to do something special with you on the day set aside for lovers?"

"Damn it, that's not fair, Jesse. If you'd told me, this never would've happened." She sank onto her haunches and pressed a fist to her mouth. Tears blurred her vision. "Now, no matter what I do, I hurt someone I love."

"Love?" He snorted. "Really, Gemma? This is how you tell me?" He pitched his voice in a mocking falsetto. "Thanks for all the trouble, but I've gotta go clubbing. By the way, I love you. Byeee."

She'd never seen his temper before. It had teeth. How to fix this?

"I'll tell them to come back later. You and I can celebrate, then they can pick me in a few hours."

His only response, a dead-eyed stare.

She sidled closer and toyed with his collar. "Really, they can wait. We could enjoy this beautiful scene, maybe fool around a little—"

"With you impatient to leave? No thanks. Go on. Be with your friends." He gave her his back, muttering, "Should've known this would never work."

"Jesse, be fair." She tugged on his sleeve. "These women are like sisters to me, and I haven't seen them in ages. They'd love to meet you. Come with us? It'll be fun."

A knock on the door interrupted her pleading. It opened a crack, and three heads peeked through. "Gemma? You okay?"

Jesse didn't turn as he whispered, "Just go."

So she did, though it took her leaden feet a thousand years to trudge to the door. Outside the green oasis, icy wind slapped her face. Too late to turn back now. She'd hurt him. He didn't want her anymore.

Her expression grave, Sierra wound her long arm around Gemma's shoulders. "Damn, did we screw things up with your new guy?"

Margot hugged her from behind. "Listen, we can go to Portland another time. Go back to him."

Olivia joined the huddle, tucking her chin onto Gemma's shoulder. "If he cares for you, he won't be jealous of your friends. That's a red flag, babe."

They didn't understand. Then again, neither did she. How could he let one disappointment erase everything they'd shared?

Caleb's gentle goodbye was a mere paper cut compared to this searing pain, but if anyone could get her through it, these three could.

She straightened her spine. "Come on, let's go have fun."

Her brain spun worse and worse imaginings all the way to Portland, but she forced a smile until her jaw ached almost as much as her gut.

Though the club's throbbing beats didn't drown out her pounding regret, at least it helped numb the ache. And if she had to flee the dance floor to catch her breath and wipe her tears, so what? Chalk it up to the crowd, the noise, the stuffy air.

It couldn't possibly be a broken heart. Hell, her heart hadn't even healed from its last stomping.

Better to just take life day by day and quit looking for soulmates. Because really, there was no such thing.

Growling to keep the tears at bay, Jesse ripped the paper hearts down and crumpled those sadistic reminders of what he'd lost. How could he have been so wrong about Gemma? She told him what she needed—excitement, passion, new experiences—and he went to a helluva lot of trouble to give it to her. But she blew him off. Their five weeks together had been a waste, a stupid distraction from what really mattered—building his business and getting on with his life.

And it's not like she didn't warn him. He knew himself well enough. To be happy, he needed to be rooted, grounded. He needed a home and loved ones he could count on. Gemma would never be satisfied with someone as dull and routine bound as him. As much as it hurt, and right now it hurt like a sonofabitch, he'd better let her go.

Grumbling curses, he packed away all the traces of his stupid romantic gesture. And his dreams of a future with Gemma.

Chapter Twelve

♥

That Valentine's Day was the most painful Gemma had ever experienced, with customer after customer skipping into the shop, hearts in their eyes, to buy love tokens for their special someone. Her pounding hangover only made things worse—why had she thought tequila would help her forget Jesse? Tequila never helped anything. And her glum silence cast a pall over breakfast and the ride home. By the time her friends dropped her off at the shop, she doubted they'd ever waste their time on her again. They felt guilty for ruining her date with Jesse. She felt guilty for choosing them over him, not that he'd left her much choice. From the moment he spotted her friends, who'd only wanted to share their love on her birthday, he'd shut down. Locked up tighter than a submarine hatch.

Happy fuckin' birthday, Gemma. Happy Valentine's Day too. The irony nauseated her.

That's what she got for hooking up with a hidebound Taurus, a jealous homebody who was too stubborn to step outside his comfort zone. She knew damn well that Taurus plus Aquarius equaled the worst match ever.

Was she being fair to categorize Jesse so quickly? Nagging guilt nibbled her conscience with sharp, ratty teeth. And fair or not, she resented him for making her feel guilty.

See? We've only been together a short time, and already I'm making myself unhappy over him. Tomorrow, I'll officially break things off. Or maybe the next day. Her integrity demanded she do it in person. She might be selfish and afraid of confinement, but she still cared about him, and probably always would. Saying goodbye to Jesse Del Toro would be agonizing.

Two days later, Zora had had enough. She flipped the shop sign to "Back in 30 minutes" and pointed to her divination station. "Behind the screen. Now."

"Here we go," Gemma muttered, bracing herself for what Zora called 'a good talking to.' No one saw through excuses and rationalizations like her psychic aunt.

Taking her sweet time, which only prolonged Gemma's torture, Zora poured them each a cup of tea, apple and cinnamon this time, with hints of orange peel and clove. She set one in front of Gemma, then sat and tented her fingers, leveling a razor-sharp stare.

Gemma sipped. "Good tea, Auntie."

"It's Jesse's recipe." Cool as the proverbial cucumber, she sipped her tea. "Haven't seen him around lately. Except when I spotted him in the supermarket yesterday. The look on his face about broke my heart. Then he scooted away in a hurry." She laid her cool hand over Gemma's trembling one. "And you've been as glum as an oyster. What happened?"

Gemma searched her tea leaves for an answer.

But Zora wasn't one to settle for silence. "You two seemed so happy together. Your combined smiles could have lit a room."

As if on cue, the shop's lights flickered.

"Big storm rolling in. The kind that blows away bad luck and washes the mind clean." She squeezed Gemma's hand. "Maybe try unburdening yourself? Let the wind carry the pain away."

"Oh Goddess." Gemma pinched her eyes shut and spilled the truth—about Jesse's Valentine surprise, his anger when she failed to choose him over her friends, her guilty self-bashing ever since. And the hopelessness that made her want to flee Trappers Cove and seek solace in new surroundings.

She swiped her tear-smeared face, her voice hoarse and tight. "He said he cared for me, but he couldn't make room in his heart for my friends. I need space to breathe, Auntie Z. Why does every guy I love want to tie me down?"

Zora patted her hand and heaved a sigh. "You're in a tough place. In this modern world, a woman's got to defend her boundaries. Putting your friends first felt like the right thing to do, didn't it?"

She nodded. "In the moment, yeah." Or as close as she could get to the right thing under those tangled circumstances.

"But to Jesse, it probably felt like goodbye."

Gemma's voice broke. "I just don't see how we can get past this. If he's hurt when I go out with friends, how's he going to feel when I need to get away for a few days? I can't put him through that over and over again. The look on his face—it tore me open, Auntie."

"Darling." Zora scooted her chair closer and put her arm around Gemma's shoulders. "You are so brilliant in some areas, but you've never been good at seeing things from another's perspective. Sounds like Jesse spent a lot of time and effort trying to please you."

Gemma knuckled her eyes. "He did, but so did my friends. How was I supposed to choose? Jesse and I were just getting started. It's not like we're married. We've never even said I love you."

"Listen to yourself, so defensive and logical." Zora tapped her sternum, making her owl pendant jingle. "Try seeing through your heart. By going to all that fuss, he was declaring his love for you."

A chill slithered over Gemma's skin as the truth coalesced, hard and brilliant as a diamond, and just as cold. Before Sunday, she and Jesse had been perched on the edge of something life changing. That fateful day, she'd nearly blurted out the big L word in a text.

He might not have said the word out loud, but his love simmered just beneath the surface, shining through every sweet gesture, every caress, every kiss. If her friends hadn't shown up in Trappers Cove, what would have happened in that magical greenhouse?

The irony stung her shredded heart like salt—the extra-chunky kind you strew on frozen sidewalks. Losing Jesse opened her eyes to how much she truly loved him. Hell, eyes open wasn't a strong enough metaphor. Knowing how badly she'd hurt him burned like being flayed alive with the dull knife of her own lunkheaded foolishness.

Despite their glaring differences, these past weeks with Jesse had been happy ones, filled with comfort and warmth, companionship and laughs and dizzying sex. Maybe he'd never forgive her, and maybe she'd killed his trust, but she couldn't surrender this sweet connection without reaching out one more time.

Please, Goddess, don't let it be too late.

"Will you excuse me, Auntie? I need to make a call." Her pounding heart rattled her bones as she stepped outside and found a quiet spot beside a planter of soggy primroses. Blustery wind tugged her hood back and peppered her face with stinging raindrops. Dropping onto the wet bench, she dialed Jesse's number and nibbled a cuticle as she waited for him to pick up. Would he? Had he blocked her?

"Gemma." His voice sounded flat. Not irritated, not angry, just—dead.

"Jesse, I—" She cleared her throat to suppress a quaver. "Listen, there's so much I want to say to you. Can I come over?"

For a long moment, all she heard was his heavy breathing. She pictured him pacing in his greenhouse, his broad shoulders hunched as he puzzled out his response.

At last, he cleared his throat. "No, Gemma. I need you to stay away. I made a mistake, hanging my hopes on you. You were up front with me about who you are and what you want out of life. I respect that. And you're right—I can't ask you to change your nature. But I'm not ready to be just another one of your friends."

Her voice broke. "Jesse, you're not. You're so much more. I'm so sorry. I should've stayed with you."

"It's too late. That night left me feeling jealous and petty. I don't like being that kind of person, but if we stick together, I'm afraid that's what I'll always be. It's no one's fault, we're simply incompatible. I wish you the best, Gemma."

He disconnected.

"Jesse, no." She crumpled over, hugging the phone to her cheek. The stinging wind stifled the sound of her sobs.

Chapter Thirteen

♥

After huddling in the rain for Goddess knows how long, Gemma finally staggered to her feet. At least she had the weather to blame for her bedraggled appearance—not that Zora would buy that excuse.

Inside, an older couple stood at the counter, tittering with her aunt over a book. As she passed, she caught a glimpse of the cover. *Kama Sutra for Seniors.*

A vision flashed in her mind's eye—her gray-haired self, in a shop like this one, ushering a laughing pair out the door and flipping the sign to Closed. Lonely and weary, future Gemma leaned her forehead against the cool glass, shut her eyes, and sighed. *Another night alone.*

The rumble of thunder yanked her back to the present.

"We'd better scoot, hon," the silver-haired gent told his lady. "Time to batten down the hatches. This storm's supposed to be a doozy."

The customers bundled up with their prize. As they left, the wind ripped the door from the man's hand and flung it wide, blowing in a spray of rain, dead leaves, and Marquetta. She shook raindrops from her slicker and reached for the security shutters' switch. "Better close up shop, love. There's a nasty storm rolling in. Library's already closed. Lots of trees down on the north side. Power outages all over."

All three of them jumped when a beer can hit the window with a loud thwack.

"Oh Lordy." Zora pulled her raincoat over her patchwork tunic and wound a scarf around her poufy hair. "Hope it's not as bad as that big blow in '16. Come on, Gemma, help me with the awnings."

"I'll handle it." The wind nearly lifted Gemma off her feet as she battled to fold up the awnings, but with the help of the real estate crew next door, she got the job done, then helped them lock down their storefront as well.

Back inside, she shook rain from her shoes. Should've worn boots today. Should've checked the weather report. Should've told Jesse how she felt before it was too late.

Marquetta threw her arm around Gemma's shoulders. "You've never been here for a winter storm, have you? This is the kind that peels roofs off buildings. Fortunately, looks like Main Street will be spared. Storm's heading southeast."

Right toward Jesse.

Her heart thundered against her ribs. Her vision narrowed. An eerie sense of prescience plucked her nerves like an ill-tuned guitar.

Maybe he'd never love her. Maybe he never really had. But he loved that farmstead, and she couldn't sit idly by waiting for the storm to wreck it. She had to help.

"I've gotta check on a friend. I'll see you both back at home." Grabbing her bag, she sprinted for her Jeep. After double-checking the doors and top were fastened down tight, she sped toward Jesse's place. Her Wrangler shuddered as blasts of wind shoved it from side to side on the winding, two-lane road. Lightning struck too damn close, throwing everything into sharp relief—gyrating trees, driving rain, lonely houses. To her left, a pine swayed and toppled into the westbound lane. With a shriek of panic, Gemma yanked the steering wheel to dodge flying branches. The Jeep spun out and teetered on two wheels before landing upright with a bone-jarring thunk. Wind howled and thunder boomed while she fought to keep her heart from bursting through her chest.

"This is crazy. I should turn back." But in her rearview mirror, she saw another pine crash to the asphalt. And another. The wind was ripping them out like weeds. No choice but to continue east.

She thanked the gods for four-wheel drive as she sloshed up Jesse's gravel road. No lights in the house or outbuildings, but headlights from three pickups illuminated the herb greenhouse. Flashlight beams danced inside, and shouting voices carried over the wind. She gaped in horror as a mighty gust lifted the greenhouse's roof. Most of it fell back into place, but one panel detached and sailed into the greenhouse to the right, smashing a hole in its side. Shards of plastic wall and torn plants flew in all directions.

Jesse's farm was disintegrating before her eyes. She wrapped her jacket tight and sprinted for the herb house, fighting the gale with every step. As she yanked the door open, a tree branch crashed onto the roof, shattering another panel.

"Jesse!" She bolted into the wreckage. At the far end, Jesse and two other men were attempting to cover an herb bed with a tarp, but vicious gusts kept ripping it from their grip. She ran to join them and grabbed the tarp's edge, hooking her fingers through the grommets. The taller blond guy nodded his thanks while the shorter, darker one weighted the tarp with bricks.

Eyes wide, Jesse spun toward her, his beautiful face contorted with fear and fury. "What the hell are you doing here?"

"I've got rope and bungee cords in the Jeep. Will that help?"

He shoved her toward the door. "Get your ass back home. It's too dangerous out here."

The guy with the bricks shook his head. "Trees are down between here and Trappers Cove. No one's getting through tonight."

She nodded. "One nearly hit me."

Jesse crossed to her in two long strides and crushed her to his chest. His voice shook. "Jesus Christ, Gemma. If you got hurt, I'd never forgive you. Or myself."

She shook too, from adrenaline and fear and the discovery that Jesse still cared for her. For one self-indulgent moment, she sank into his embrace and held on tight. Perhaps it wasn't too late to change his mind. But this was not the time to delve into regrets and apologies, not with a greenhouse to save.

"The storm's nobody's fault, Jesse." She wriggled from his grip. "Put me to work."

He cupped her jaw with dirt-smeared hands. "Why did you come?"

"Because you were in frickin' danger! And I still have feelings for you, okay? Now tell me what to do."

Working side by side with Ryan, owner of the Salty Dog Saloon, and Ben, a nearby farmer, they covered the most vulnerable plants, patched the roof as best they could with plywood and tarps, then cranked up generators to keep the herbs from freezing. Hours later, it seemed, Jesse thanked his friends and sent them home. Ryan, who lived in town, went with Ben, who had a wood stove and generator.

"We'll be back in the morning." Ryan gave Jesse a brotherly arm punch. "So you better have a huge stack of pancakes waiting."

"I'll bring the bacon," Ben added.

"Wow." Gemma wiped dirt from her sweaty forehead as she watched them drive away. "Those guys must really love you."

"Guess so." Jesse rotated his shoulder and winced. "Ryan was out here trying to talk sense into my mopey ass. Ben called to warn us about the storm. We drove out to his place and made sure all the animals were secure in the barns. The sheep were panicked, running everywhere. If it weren't for his dogs, he'd have lost the whole flock." He leaned against a raised bed and heaved a sigh. "By the time we got back here, the wind was ripping the greenhouses like paper. The flower house is probably a total loss, but at least this one will stand."

She peered through a ragged gap in the wall. "Wind's dying down a little."

He took her hand and kissed her knuckles. "From your lips to God's ear. Come on." He pushed the door open and tugged her through. "Let's get you dry."

The house was pitch dark, but Jesse lit candles before going to the back porch and returned with an armload of firewood. Crouched at the hearth, he poked the kindling until flames rose, then sank onto the floor, his elbows on his knees.

In the spirit of making herself useful, as well as avoiding the awkward silence, Gemma fetched towels from the hallway closet. "Here." Shivering, she knelt and blotted his dripping hair. "Want me to get you some dry clothes?"

"In a minute." He stared into the fire.

A gust shook the windowpanes. The old house creaked under nature's assault.

Finally, with a huge sigh, Jesse turned and met her eye. "I'm still mad at you."

"I know." She reached for the buttons of his shirt. "You have every right to be. I have a bone to pick with you too. But for now, can we please dry off?"

"Fair enough." He slowly unfolded his large frame and tugged her to her feet. They trudged to the bedroom, where he flicked on the overhead lamp.

"Electricity's back?"

He snorted. Goddess, she'd missed that sound.

"Propane generator. Fired it up when I got the firewood. We'll have lights and running water, at least. Here." He rummaged in his dresser and tossed her a flannel shirt, a pair of sweatpants, and thick woolen socks. "You can change in there." He pointed to the bathroom, turned his back, and stripped off his dripping shirt.

"Jesse, you've already seen every inch of me."

"Well, I don't want to see it now."

Her heart shriveled.

With a grunt, he slammed the drawer. "Don't need lust clouding my judgment. That's how we got into this mess in the first place."

In the bathroom, she shed her wet garments, blotted her sopping hair, and pulled on Jesse's clothes, warm and soft against her bare skin. The plaid flannel shirt nearly reached her knees, but since he was so averse to seeing her body, she stepped into the sweats and cinched the waist tight. The socks were ridiculously large, too, but better than padding through the cold house in bare feet. Borrowing his comb, she unsnarled her mane before stepping into the bedroom.

"Jesse?" No sign of him, but a fire crackled in the fireplace.

"How freakin' romantic," she muttered, bitterness sharp on her tongue.

She found him in the kitchen stirring two mugs of hot cocoa. When she approached, he turned and wordlessly held up a bottle of Jameson.

"Yes, please."

He added a generous glug to each mug, handed her one, and beckoned her to the living room, where he sat on the sofa and patted the cushion beside him.

Nerves wound tight, she sat and curled her legs beneath her.

He wrapped the worn sofa quilt around their shoulders, then gave her a long, narrow-eyed stare. His jaw muscles worked. She could almost see the wheels turning in his skull—tick, tick, tick.

He crossed his arms, making his biceps bulge. Unfair—how was she supposed to concentrate?

"My gramps had a saying about how people are like tea bags. You don't find out how strong they are until they land in hot water." He reached for his mug.

She did the same, taking a big gulp of sugary liquid courage before twisting to face him. "Look, Jesse. I am what I am. Flawed, impulsive, insensitive."

Jesse nodded, his expression solemn.

Throw me a crumb, will you? She took another sip and plowed ahead. "And you're flawed too. Jealous when there's no need, stubborn, and far too Netflix and chill for my taste."

"Hmmph." His lips quirked to the side.

She laid her hand on his knee. "But here's the thing—I've felt more alive, more myself these past weeks with you than I have in a long time. Flitting from place to place scratches an itch in my soul. I don't know how to reconcile that with loving a man who's deeply rooted to one place—even if it's a town as magical as Trappers Cove."

Jesse's hand closed over hers. His eyebrows unclenched. "Did you say loving?"

Her belly fluttered, but she raised her chin and faced her fear. "Yes. I love you, Jesse Del Toro. And that's terrifying, because being tied down to one place makes me..."

"Itchy?" He cocked an eyebrow. "Or do you just hate being tied to one person?"

"No." With a firm head shake, she took his face in both hands, loving the scratchy softness of his beard against her palms. "I don't feel that way about you. In fact, I'm ninety-nine point nine, nine, nine percent sure you're the one. My person. Isn't it weird that fate would send me the least compatible man imaginable and make him so completely irresistible that I have to rethink everything?"

Jesse's gaze softened. He enfolded her hand in his warm, work-roughened palms. "I don't want you to rethink everything, Gemma. I just want you to be mine. And if I have to let you go wander sometimes, I can live with that. I'll be edgy the whole time you're gone, but I'll endure it for your sake."

She dropped a kiss into his palm. "How about coming with me?"

A huge grin spread his lips. "If I can get someone to watch the greenhouses, yeah. Sometimes I'll come with you." He wrapped her in his strong arms and pressed his forehead to hers. "I don't want you to change your nature, Gemma. I find your nature intoxicating."

The glow in her chest obliterated the howling storm outside, the fears holding her back, and every last defense that stood between her and her prize—Jesse Del Toro's love. Arm in arm, heart to heart, they'd figure out a way to make this star-crossed connection shine bright and strong and true.

Jesse gathered her against his chest and nuzzled her hair. "You know what I want now, more than anything?"

She arched her breasts against him, wishing he'd get on with it already. "I want that too, Jesse."

"Perfect." Grinning, he pressed his forehead to hers. "Bubbles or no bubbles?"

"Huh?"

"You're still shivering." He ran his hands up and down her arms. "Let's warm up in the bath."

"Oh." Disappointment popped her happy, horny bubble, until she realized what a bath with Jesse would probably entail. Warm, relaxed muscles, slippery skin, squeaky clean manly bits ready for her delectation. Grinning, she ran her fingertip over his whiskered jaw. "You pick."

His feral grin glinted in the firelight. "I love it when you let me take charge."

"Hmmm." Her fingertip traced spirals over his chest. "I noticed that."

His fiery gaze pinned her for a long, heated moment. His nostrils flared, and he clutched the back of her head and claimed a searing kiss—sweet, hot, and a bit chocolaty. Absolutely delicious.And then he released her.

Whimpering, she reached for him.

"Patience, love." He rose to his feet and backed away, wearing a devilish grin. "I'll fetch you when it's time."

She curled on the couch, lulled by the thrum of rain and wind and the fire's crackling counterpoint. She was on the verge of drifting off to sleep when she felt hot breath on her cheek. "Your bath is ready. Let's go." His strong arms tunneled beneath her body and lifted her into the air.

"Jesse," she squeaked, almost ashamed of how much this clichéd gesture turned her on. Sailing down the hall cradled against her man's chest was all kinds of delightful.

In the bathroom, he set her feet on the fluffy rug, grasped the hem of her borrowed shirt, and whipped it over her head. His hands smoothed over her sides, down her back to rest on the swell of her ass. "I didn't think I'd ever touch your satin skin again. I'm so glad you came back."

She flattened her palms on his broad chest and gazed into his whiskey brown eyes. "I'll always come back to you, Jesse. Wherever you are, that's my home." She gave his collar a clumsy yank. Must've been more alcohol in those drinks than she'd realized. Good thing his flannel shirt fastened with snaps and not buttons.

Running her hands all over his bare torso was almost as heavenly as the pleasure to come. She'd missed this strong, solid man, the sensual contrast between his smooth skin and the coarse hair across his muscular chest and belly.

"Damn, woman, you sure can tie a knot." Grumbling like a horny bear, Jesse tugged on the drawstring of her borrowed sweatpants.

"How 'bout I do mine and you do yours?" Giggling, she slithered out of the giant sweats while Jesse unfastened his jeans and let them fall to the floor.

His fat, ruddy cock rose to greet her. She reached for him with greedy hands.

"Ah, ah, ah, bath first." With a teasing smile, he climbed into the oversize tub, spread his knees wide, and waggled his eyebrows.

Stepping carefully, she settled between his splayed legs and rested her back against his hot, muscly chest. Thoughtful man, he'd stocked up on her favorite soap from Zora's shop, a fresh, herbal scent with rosemary, eucalyptus, and mint. He lathered up his big hands and stroked them over every inch of her body while she purred and stretched.

"Turn around, Gemma."

Giggling, she hugged her knees to her chest and spun on her behind so he could massage her feet and run his strong fingers between her toes, leaving her weak and giddy with pleasure. Leave it to Jesse to reveal yet another erogenous zone.

"Your turn, love." She wrapped her legs around his waist and gave him the same slow, sensuous soaping, taking her time to relish every curve and plane from his neck to his powerful legs. When she soaped his feet, he squirmed and laughed, sloshing water onto the floor.

Ticklish, eh? She filed that away for future use.

Saving the best bit for last, she skimmed past his tempting cock and reached for a plastic pitcher on the tub's rim. "Tilt your head back."

She sluiced warm water over his head, then filled her palm with shampoo and lathered his thick curls, massaging in firm circles with the pads of her fingers.

"Ahhh." His eyes closed on a sigh, and his head lolled onto her shoulder. "You really do have magic powers, don't you?"

She rinsed away the suds and lathered her hands again for the pièce de résistance. His hips bucked as soon as she gripped his rigid shaft. Well, that part certainly hadn't relaxed. When she gently cupped his balls, he whimpered, then scooped her up by her armpits and tugged the plug away with his toes. "Time for bed."

He unfolded a big, fluffy towel—because of course Jesse made sure each sensuous detail was perfect—and dried her in firm strokes. She'd only halfway dried his big body when, eyes aflame, he whisked the towel from her hands, lifted her into his arms, and carried her to the bed.

"You better not drop me, mister."

With a sexy snarl, he nibbled her neck, then tossed her onto the mattress. Laughing, he dove on top of her and wrapped her with his arms and legs. "You should have seen your tits bounce. Magnificent."

Laughing and tickling, they wrestled until he sprawled atop her, one leg between hers, his cock throbbing against her belly, his fingers tangled in her hair.

"Gemma. So beautiful." His smile melted into a gaze of reverence. Never had she felt more cherished.

He rose onto his elbow and twined a damp strand around his finger. "Is it true? Do you really love me?"

"I do, Jesse." She wound her arms around his neck. "Now come to me."

"Hallelujah." He opened the nightstand drawer, sheathed himself, then covered her hungry body with his, sliding against her until her nerve endings crackled and flashed. Nimble fingers parted her folds, settling on her hyper-sensitized clit.

She arched on a moan. The emotion of the day swam just under her skin. Swirling together with this heady arousal, the mixture threatened to combust.

"Please, Jesse," she gasped. "I need you inside me."

He entered her in one slow glide, stretching and filling her until she wanted to weep and sing and hold him this close forever. No games this time, no teasing, just undulating in each other's arms, his pleasure twining with hers, spinning them higher and higher until he shouted her name, and she clasped him so tight, bliss wiping away every fear, every thought but *Jesse, Jesse, Jesse.*

Afterward, she lay in his arms, happy and content, one hundred percent sure she'd made the right choice. It wouldn't be easy, finding a way to join their contrasting natures, but their connection was strong enough, sweet enough, true enough to last.

Chapter Fourteen

♥

After circling the vendors' parking lot at the Portland Expo Hall again and again, Jesse finally found a spot for his truck. He secured a tarp over his rolling cart to protect his tender plant babies, survivors of last week's storm, from the wicked wind. He'd hoped to contribute much more to this event, but even with the help of a dozen friends, he was only able to salvage about half his crop after repairing the greenhouses.

He texted Gemma.

Here. Where's your booth, love?

Aisle Five, halfway down

The Esoteric Arts Expo had started two hours ago, but an emergency call from Francesca's restaurant delayed his arrival. At least his ladies weren't late to the party. And what a party! The cavernous hall was bursting with woo-woo types from flower-crowned hippie grandparents to tiny kids in home-spun sweaters. He rolled his cart past vendors selling kombucha and kimchi, past-life regression, aura readjustment, enough jewelry for multiple dragon hoards, and every CBD product known to man, not to mention all the tie-dyed, bejeweled, funky clothing.

And he'd thought his borrowed Renn faire shirt and Celtic knot necklace would fit right in. Ha! He felt positively bland among all these crystal-bead-fairy types.

He spotted Zora's purple fortune-teller tent from Trappers Cove's July Fourth bash. She'd even brought her crystal ball. Probably just a prop, but you never knew with Zora. Her elaborately carved chair sat empty, though, and a sign on the tent flap read *The Seer will be back in ten minutes.*

Gemma hadn't seen him yet, so he took a moment to drink in the sight of his ladylove in her element. Dressed in a long velvet gown, a flowered crown over her loose, wavy hair, she made a perfect Maid Marian. Hmm, maybe some costumed role play? He added a mental note to his Keeping Gemma Interested file.

As she bent to ring up a handful of crystals, her dress gaped at the neckline, displaying her creamy cleavage. His inner bull snorted, riled at the idea of all these shoppers ogling his woman.

He shoved the beast back into its stall and rolled his cart behind the table. "Morning, beautiful."

"Jesse!" Her smile shone brighter than all those crystal doodads as she threw her arms around his neck and rose on tiptoe to kiss him.

"Sorry I'm late. Francesca had a basil emergency."

She patted his chest. "I'll bet she just wanted to ogle the herb farmer. Love the shirt. You're quite the swashbuckler." With a sexy little growl, she swirled her fingertip in his chest hair.

Joy filled him like sunshine. God, he loved this woman.

"C'mon." She tugged him to the display. "Come see what Marquetta made."

The table was piled high with cellophane packets holding teas, smudge sticks, bath salts, plus herb-infused massage oils, lip balms, and hand creams, all emblazoned with colorful labels reading *Del Toro Botanicals*.

"I scoured the internet to find the perfect bull. He looks just like you, my sexy beast."

Jesse squinted at the image, then threw back his head and roared with laughter. If Gemma thought he resembled this curly-haired brute with fiery eyes and steam shooting out its snout, he wasn't about to argue with her.

"The logo is awesome." He kissed the tip of her nose. "I'm truly flattered. Where should I unload the plants?"

She pointed to a wooden shelf, then turned her attention to a customer. He finished unloading in time to hear her say, "Del Toro Botanicals, our partner for organic herbs, was a victim of last week's storm." She tapped a large jar half-filled with coins and bills. "Any help you can give to the rebuilding fund would be much appreciated."

The old hippie dude dumped his change into the jar.

"You made a tip jar for me?" He peered at the label, a photo of his hodgepodge crew of helpers in front of the decimated greenhouses.

She shrugged. "The aunties and I want to do what we can to help."

"Gemma, you are the best." Tears prickled his eyes as he pulled her to his chest and rocked her, heedless of the crowd.

Zora and Marquetta arrived with a tray of chai lattes, interrupting their embrace. "Oh," Marquetta cooed. "Look at the lovebirds. It warms my old heart to see you two back together." She set down the drinks and threw her arms around both of them.

Zora joined the hug scrum too. "I love our little family," she sighed into Jesse's back.

Jesse grinned so hard his cheeks ached. All the help he received from Trappers Cove this past week proved they really were much more than neighbors—they were the best kind of family, connected by bonds stronger than blood. Adding Gemma to his clan of the heart was the crowning touch. He truly was a happy man.

"Okay, enough mushy stuff." Marquetta released him and rubbed her palms together. "Show us your surprise, Jesse."

"Right." He blotted his eyes on his sleeve. "I found this collection of old pots in the rubble. Gramps must've used them for decorative plants back in the day." He'd cleaned up the ceramic pots, big and small, shallow and deep, and filled them with whatever herb plants he could salvage after the storm. With a homemade stencil and gold spray paint, he labeled each *Good Vibes Garden*. Hand-lettered popsicle sticks identified the herbs in each pot.

"Didn't have time to research all their magical properties, but I figure you ladies can explain that part to customers."

The three women couldn't have looked happier if he'd presented them with a basket of kittens. Gemma clapped a hand over her heart. "But you don't believe in this woo-woo stuff."

Jesse shrugged. "Not really, but you do, and that's good enough for me." He took her hand and kissed it. "Thank you for showing this stubborn ass a way to expand his market."

Gemma snuggled into his arms. "And thank you for helping me expand my—well, everything. You taught me something important about myself."

"What's that?"

"The value of roots. Guess I had to fall in love with a farmer to learn that lesson." She pressed her soft lips to his.

Honestly, if she kept on kissing him like this, both his heart and his dick were going to explode.

She purred into his ear, "Of course, I'll always crave new experiences. It's my Aquarius nature, you know."

He squeezed her hip. "Woman, you and your new experiences are going to wear me out. What do you have in mind?"

She giggled. "You look mighty fine in that pirate shirt. How about adding an eye patch?"

He gave her a mock-stern glare. "Okay. But I draw the line at a parrot."

She laughed into his kiss. "Agreed. The only one I want to hear squawking in our bed is you."

"Ahem." A middle-aged couple in medieval garb stood at the table. "We're ready for our reading."

"Of course you are, darlings," Zora cooed, smoothing her velvet caftan. "Come in, have a seat." She ushered them into her tent and closed the curtain.

While Jesse enjoyed his spicy latte, Gemma tended to customers, charming them with in-depth knowledge of her woo-woo wares. Grinning like a kid on Christmas morning, he watched her work the crowd. Loving Gemma was a huge risk, but she'd taught him a valuable lesson—if you want to fly, you've gotta take a leap of faith. And he was so glad he'd jumped.

"C'mon, Jesse." She beckoned, a wicked twinkle in her eye. "Put those big, strong hands to use." She handed him a bottle of massage oil, then tilted her head toward a pair of women eyeing the merchandise.

Did she really mean...?

"I dare you," she whispered.

Okay then. If she wanted a show, he'd give her one.

He pitched his voice low and seductive. "Hello, ladies. Care to sample our organically sourced herbal massage oil? I grow the herbs with these very hands." He squirted some into his palm. "If you roll up your sleeve, ma'am, I'll show you how it tingles."

Mesmerized, both women thrust their arms forward.

Gemma elbowed him and shot him a smile brimming with sexy mischief. New experiences, huh? He had a feeling this woo-woo stuff could be fun.

As he massaged the customers' wrists, Zora's voice carried from her fortune-telling tent. "I understand your trepidations. Normally, your zodiac signs aren't the most auspicious combination. But, my darlings, love can be stronger than the stars. If you respect each other's individuality, I see a bright future ahead of you."

Thanks for reading **Passion in the Cards**! If you enjoyed Jesse and Gemma's story, please leave a review on Goodreads.

Don't miss the next steamy story in the **Trappers Cove** series. Check out Ryan and Lilo's story, **Passionate Brew: An Enemies-to-Lovers Beach Town Brewery Romance.** When a control-freak brewery owner is forced to partner with a prickly, seductive master brewer, their business and their hearts will never be the same.

Author's Note and Acknowledgments

One of the many things I love about writing fiction is the chance to explore all the careers I might have pursued if my life had taken a different turn. So far, I've written about running a bookshop (*Through the Red Door*), an ice cream shop (*Gelato Surprise*), an art/photography studio (*Runaway Love Story, Love, Art, and Other Obstacles*), a tattoo studio (*Opposites Ignite)* a neighborhood bar (*Bangers Tavern Romance series*), a food-truck (*Delicious Heat*), and now a hippie-dippy shop and an herb farm!

I owe a huge thanks to the many professionals who answer my pesky questions, and to all the YouTubers who provide virtual tours of their businesses and passions.

Thanks to Dar Albert of Wicked Smart Designs for her inspired book covers, and to my oh-so-patient husband for supporting me in my writing journey. He says I'm the only wife he knows who encourages her husband to go play golf so she can write uninterrupted. You're the BHE, Babes!

Books by Sadira Stone

♥

The Bangers Tavern Romance Series

Sizzling contemporary romance set in a neighborhood bar in Tacoma, Washington. Found family, all the feels, and the best tater tots in town!

<u>Christmas Rekindled: Bangers Tavern Romance One</u>

Bangers' bartender River has a damn good reason for hating Christmas, and an equally good reason for resenting new server Charlie—until a kiss under the mistletoe flares hot enough to melt the North Pole. To save the bar they love, these two Scrooges must put aside their enmity and find the good in each other. Enemies to lovers, fake dating, workplace romance

<u>Opposites Ignite: Bangers Tavern Romance Two</u>

A mismatch sparks the hottest flames! Bodacious, curvy, blue-haired, aspiring tattoo artist Rosie is too smart to fall for her strait-laced coworker at Bangers Tavern. But his shy smile and quiet charm disarm her defenses just when she needs them most. Curvy heroine, shy hero, opposites attract, workplace romance

Delicious Heat: Bangers Tavern Romance Three

Bangers Tavern chef Diego meets a woman who makes his heart sing. Trouble is, she's pregnant with another man's child. To win her, he'll have to convince her and both their interfering families that he's in it for keeps. Foodie romance, pregnant heroine, chef hero, forbidden love, sassy abuela

Sweet Slow Sizzle: Bangers Tavern Romance Four

Bangers Tavern's hunky bouncer Jojo has been crushing on server Lana for years, but her sole focus is keeping her orphaned teen brothers together in the only home they've ever known. When their teen shenanigans land them in trouble, Jojo may be the only person who can save them. Friends to lovers, slow burn, single "mom," workplace romance

Cupid's Silver Spark: A Bangers Tavern Romance Novella

Will Cupid's misfire cost her everything? Still stinging from a breakup, Carla Portofino reluctantly lets her bestie drags her to Bangers Tavern's Anti-Valentine's Bash, Cupid gifts her a swoonworthy silver fox. Maybe a no-strings fling is the remedy for her tattered heart? He seems perfect, until a greedy real estate development scheme tangles them in more string than either can handle. Over-40 romance, Valentine's Day, lovers to enemies to lovers

The Book Nirvana Series

Steamy contemporary romance set in a quirky bookshop in Eugene, Oregon—because bookshops are sexy!

<u>Through the Red Door: Book Nirvana One</u>

Widow Clara struggles to keep her indie bookshop afloat. Professor Nick comes in search of historical erotica from her famed collection but stays for the lovely bookseller--until a scandal from his past shatters her trust. Love triangle, widowed heroine and hero, second chance at love.

<u>Runaway Love Story: Book Nirvana Two</u>

Fierce passion or long-cherished dreams—she can't hang onto both. An ambitious artist and a sweet, hunky beta hero face family secrets, clashing dreams, and a social media storm, armed only with sizzling chemistry and a strange feeling each might be The One. City Mouse/Country Mouse, athletes, cinnamon roll hero.

<u>Love, Art, and Other Obstacles: Book Nirvana Three</u>

Two young artists—one prickly and independent, one cocky and flirtatious—compete for a prize that could jump-start their careers. Their surprise connection sizzles, but can he battle past her defenses and prove he loves her as she is? Rivals to lovers, bisexual heroine, grumpy/sunshine.

<u>Gelato Surprise, a standalone beach romance novella</u>

When her dastardly ex spoils their family vacation, Danielle heads to the beach alone to lick her wounds. Dashing young gelato vendor Matteo is too delicious to resist. He's determined to make their vacation fling last beyond summer, but convincing her he can fit into her life will take much more than sweet treats and summer kisses. Older woman/younger man, divorced heroine, summer fling.

About the Author

♥

Award-winning contemporary romance author Sadira Stone spins steamy, smoochy tales set in small businesses—a quirky bookstore, a neighborhood bar, a vintage boutique... Her stories highlight found family, friendship, and the sizzling chemistry that pulls unlikely partners together. When she emerges from her writing cave in Las Vegas, Nevada, which she seldom does, she enjoys dance classes, strumming her ukulele, exploring the West with her charming husband, cooking up a storm, and gobbling all the romance books. For a guaranteed HEA (and no cliffhangers!) visit Sadira at .

Visit Sadira on All the Socials!
https://linktr.ee/SadiraStone

www.ingramcontent.com/pod-product-compliance
Lightning Source LLC
Chambersburg PA
CBHW021735190726
48288CB00009B/3060